T0208328

MYSTERY AT SKY MOUNTAIN

BILL KNOWLES

authorHOUSE®

AuthorHouse™
1663 Liberty Drive
Bloomington, IN 47403
www.authorhouse.com
Phone: 833-262-8899

Published by AuthorHouse 10/04/2023

ISBN: 979-8-8230-0903-4 (sc)
ISBN: 979-8-8230-0908-9 (e)

Library of Congress Control Number: 2023909836

Print information available on the last page.

This book is printed on acid-free paper.

CONTENTS

CHAPTER 1

MYSTERIOUS CALLER

"Who could that be at this time of the morning?" Luke Robinson went to the hall to answer the phone. "Maybe a call from Uncle Tom." said Bobby rubbing his eyes. "It can't be Mom and Dad they are on board a cruise." Luke answered the phone, "Hello?" The caller on the other end replied in a deep voice, *Sky Mountain is the key to the puzzle*". Then the caller hung up.

"What was that all about?" Bobby asked in suspense.

Luke paced the room and thought for a moment. He replied. "The caller said the key to the puzzle is at Sky Mountain."

"What puzzle?" Bobby quizzed him.

Luke shrugged "Search me."

"Well then who was the caller?" Bobby said.

"I don't know that, either" Luke said, perplexed. "He didn't stay on the phone long enough for me to ask but I heard the ocean in the background." Bobby got out of bed and opened his laptop. He searched the web for Sky Mountain and its history.

"It says here Sky Mountain means Mountains of Heaven and was formed about a thousand years ago. It is full of caves and that the pioneers used them when westward expansion exploded in the early 1800's."

The boys, twins at birth and nineteen years old, decided to take a trip to Sky Mountain the next day at sunset to scope out the area after dinner when the weather was a little cooler. After dinner both boys grabbed their cellphones, and some Gatorade then went out to their Mustang convertible.

Looking up directions to Sky Mountain they headed out. Luke said, "Should take us about an hour to get there." About a half hour into the trip the boys discovered that there is a shorter way to get there and turned off the exit. The boys kept a sharp lookout for the street sign when suddenly Bobby noticed the turning lane and slammed on the brakes.

"If I had not noticed that turn lane, we would have totally missed it." Bobby groaned.

A few miles down the road they came to a roadblock.

"Oh, no! A barricade!" Luke said angrily.

"That's weird," Bobby murmured. "There's no sign as to why the road is cutoff and I see no road crews."

"Maybe they forgot to remove the sign and the road is actually okay to travel." Luke said hopefully.

"Let's take a chance." Bobby said.

He hopped out and removed the sawhorse and sign.

"Keep your fingers crossed this works," Bobby said.

"I would hate for something to happen to the car and my cell battery run out and we have no idea how to get out of here." Luke said with a worried expression. Bobby jumped back in the car and they both proceeded cautiously.

The boys continued their journey down the dirt road

looking for any clues. Ahead, the road was full of twists and turns. At various times both boys looked at each other with cautious optimism. *Was this possibly a trick being played on them they wondered?*

After several minutes the boys were puzzled not to see any sign of buildings. Or why the roadblock had been set up.

"Maybe we should have turned again" Luke said.

Bobby was about to answer when both brothers were startled to see a shiny object just up ahead and what appeared to be a light beacon on top of it. He slammed on the brakes and the car skidded crazily then came to a halt up on a steep hill that bordered the road.

Luke jumped out and investigated what was the source of the light. It was some sort of old safe that looked to have been built back in the 1920's and assumed the safe was locked. He tried the handle anyway.

His luck was with him today as the handle turned and the safe opened. It was full of papers, coins, and hard drive discs from a company called Pioneer.

"That's strange," Bobby murmured. "We find papers near a mountain that was visited by pioneers, and we had Pioneer Corporation here in town."

Luke put his hand on his chin. "Maybe it's just a coincidence."

"Let's take the papers and discs with us and find out more about this company." said Bobby.

"Didn't Dad work with the CEO of Pioneer to try and save the company about five years ago?" Bobby asked.

"That's right he did" Luke said.

Ted Robinson, the boys' father, was a former agent with the CIA. After retiring from the agency, he settled in Mclean, VA to become a private analyst. Bobby and Luke, who seemed to have their father's knack for investigative work, often aided him in his research investigations. The brothers had solved their first mystery, *The Ghost Machine*, and most recently, the strange *Mystery at Falls Point*. Now on summer vacation from college the boys were hoping to gain an assignment from their father once he and their mother returned from their cruise to the Caribbean.

Suddenly Luke had a terrorizing thought and looked at Bobby quizzically.

"This thing has a beacon light on it which means somebody must be looking for it either from the air or headed this way" he told Bobby as he collected the papers and disc drives.

"You're right but do we wait to see who might show up?" Bobby inquired.

"Let's turn around and find a secluded spot to hide the car." Luke proposed. They hid the treasure in the trunk and hopped back in the car. They turned around and found an area of bushes to hide the mustang. Overhead the boys could hear a buzzing sound and looked all around to find the source.

"That sounds like a drone." whispered Luke.

Bobby nodded in agreement and concluded whoever was at the controls could not be that far away.

Suddenly the drone appeared overhead, and the boys could hear sounds coming from down the road.

"The drone is coming right over top of us." Bobby said with terror in his voice.

We better get out of here fast!" Luke whispered.

But before either of the boys could move, a new sound captured their attention. Car tires could be heard in the distance, and it was heading this way. Luckily both boys hid themselves and the car well.

Within minutes a black Audi appeared and stopped near the spot where the safe was located.

Two men jumped out of the car and headed toward the safe.

Bobby and Luke struggled to see who it was that got out of the car. Two men dressed in black shirts and pants approached the safe.

Suddenly Bobby's phone rang, and he quickly tried to silence the ringer. Luke looked on with horror as the two men stopped in their tracks and turned to look in their direction. The drone was now directly overhead of the two men and the safe. Luke could faintly hear the men talking in the distance.

"I thought I heard a phone ring!" the stranger sounded.

"Nah, it was the drone you were hearing" the other man retorted.

Both men opened the safe and looked inside. To their dismay they discovered only the coins.

"Somebody's beaten us to the job!" the taller man shouted. Just then the man got out his iPhone and placed a call.

"The papers and discs aren't here." Luke overheard the man say faintly.

"I don't know, no one knows it's here. Max and I just got here."

Now Luke knew the name of at least one of the men standing near the safe.

Suddenly the drone started to circle the area and both boys were sure they would be spotted. Luckily the sun was setting, and the falling darkness covered their hideout. No sooner had the boys settled flat on the ground into their hideout than the drone passed overhead of their location with a high pitch squeal.

The drone hovered overhead, and the boys realized they had been spotted. They suddenly felt woozy and blacked out. Several minutes had passed before they awoke and discovered the drone and the Audi had vanished.

Bobby was the first to get up off the ground and look around his surroundings. Luke stirred and with a mighty effort got up to join Bobby.

"Are you okay?" asked Luke weakly.

"I feel like I got cross checked into the boards." Bobby groaned.

Both boys had played hockey locally and were star defensemen for their travel teams growing up in Virginia.

As they cleared the cobwebs in their heads, the brothers realized that their car was searched but nothing was taken.

Luke froze with fear about what was hidden in the trunk.

They went to open the trunk and discovered the papers, and the disk drives were gone.

"Who was flying that drone I wonder." said Luke.

"I don't know," Bobby answered. "If they were connected to those men then they must have met up with them after they knocked us out cold."

"Let's go check and see if the safe is still there." Luke said excitedly.

Both boys went in search of the safe and discovered it was still there.

It was open and the beacon light was missing.

"They took what was left in the safe as well." Luke said disappointed. They turned on their cellphone flashlights and searched all around the area to see if perhaps the men had dropped any clues.

Walking back to their car Bobby discovered one of the discs on the ground.

"Look what I found!" Bobby said excitedly. "They must have been in such a hurry that they didn't notice it fell to the ground."

Bobby put the disc in his pocket and continued to search the area all around the safe and then headed back to their car.

As they approached their car, they discovered surprisingly that there was no damage to their car even though it had been searched.

"Did you get a picture on your phone of either of the men?" Bobby asked Luke.

"I got two photos', but I think they were too far away, and I couldn't use the flash for fear of being discovered." Luke said dejected as he looked at his phone.

"What about the Audi license plate?" Bobby asked.

"Too far away" Luke said.

Suddenly the boys froze as they heard dogs barking in the distance.

"Do you hear what I hear?" Luke whispered.

"Yes, listen!"

Someone was talking loudly on their phone as the sounds got louder and louder. Both boys stared off in the distance but couldn't see anything.

Are we on somebody's property, Bobby wondered?

They switched off their flashlights and crouched down behind some bushes and waited.

From nearby the sound got louder with the sound of footsteps on leaves. A man and his son appeared with two large dogs on leashes who bared their teeth.

The boys froze in their tracks.

"What are you doing on my property?" the stranger snapped. He shined the light in both boys' eyes waving it back and forth.

"Please turn off the light and we will explain." Luke pleaded.

The stranger shined the light on the ground in lieu of turning it off just in case the boys decided to make a run for it. Bobby decided to play innocent and gauge if the stranger was really the owner or with the group of men who attacked them.

"Our car stalled out and we had no idea where we are."

Luke played along with his brother knowing his plan of attack.

"Can you tell us what town we are in?"

The stranger eyed both boys and spoke in low tones with his son.

They decided that the boys were not telling the truth.

"Both of you are trespassing and I should call the cops" he argued.

Bobby realized the man could be telling the truth and not aware of any safe.

"We are leaving, there is no need to do that." Luke pleaded.

The stranger and his son backed up and had their guns at their side. Bobby and Luke walked to their car and got in and started the engine. Moments later they were on the highway.

The next morning, after staying up late to discuss the case, the brothers wanted to know more about Pioneer Corporation. They set up a meeting with a family friend whom their father trusted and could shine a little light on the situation. After arriving at the offices of Peterson & Associates they were escorted into the spacious offices of the CEO, Douglas Peterson.

Doug was a gray haired, distinguished-looking man who arose from behind a grand mahogany desk and extended his hand in greeting.

"Boys, come on in, it's great to see you". He pointed out for them to take seats and offered them a beverage.

The tall executive listened intently as the boys described what happened up near Sky Mountain beginning with the strange call.

"Pioneer Corporation was a very successful company in the mid 90's. It's a shame that it closed its doors under mysterious circumstances."

Bobby and Luke showed Doug the disc that they found

in the abandoned safe and talked about the two men who showed up.

"It's strange how you get a call about Sky Mountain and the next day those men show up as well." Doug offered.

The tall executive sat back in his chair and thought for a moment. Finally, with a grin on his face, "I think you boys finally have another case. A new company started up shortly after Pioneer shut down, which raised a few eyebrows."

"What company is that Mr. Peterson?" Bobby inquired.

"A company called Advanced Analytics" Doug answered.

"Never heard of them, but maybe our father has."

The Robinsons listened intently as he related the story of how Pioneer Corporation came to end and how Advanced Analytics came to be. The firm was a nationwide provider of broad range data services to startup companies and is based in Fairfax.

"What is Advanced Analytics?" Bobby queried.

"And how does it connect to Pioneer?" Luke jumped in

Doug explained that Advanced Analytics is an umbrella term for a group of high-level methods and tools that can help you get more out of your data. He further explained that the predictive capabilities of advanced analytics can be used to forecast trends, events, and behaviors.

"Let me take a look at that disc?" Doug asked.

"Can you analyze what might be on it?" Bobby asked.

Bobby gave the disc to Doug, and he put it into his computer. The disc immediately locked out and needed a code key.

"This doesn't surprise me and may take some time." said Doug.

"How will we find the code key?" Bobby said dejectedly.

"I will get our IT folks to see if they can get in." he said sounding hopeful. He did not want to dash the boys' hopes.

"Let's grab some lunch and talk it over so more." Doug smiled.

CHAPTER 2

DOUBLE DUTY

Doug took the boys to lunch at a local restaurant, and they talked more about Pioneer Corporation.

"What exactly happened at Pioneer?" Luke asked.

"Pioneer was a startup company founded by Greg Gaines. The company wanted to sell newly designed onboard navigation systems for private jet companies." Doug answered.

"I read that the company's stock soared." Luke replied.

"It did Luke and then the logistics plans were somehow stolen from the inside. These plans were never recovered, and the company went under." Doug replied.

"But then the CEO was killed in some plane crash I read." said Bobby

"Yes," Doug answered. "The plane was never found, and I'm convinced that the only way that case will get solved is if somebody works on the inside. This is where I think you boys could help solve this whole mystery." replied Doug.

The tall executive studied the boys' faces for a moment. "I

think I know someone who could help us and make plans for you to be hired as mailroom attendees at Advanced Analytics for the summer. When are your mother and father due back from their trip?" Doug inquired.

"Their ship gets into Baltimore on Saturday." said Bobby.

"Good, then I would like us to bring your father up to speed on this."

"I agree." Luke said with a smile.

The boys shook hands with Doug outside the restaurant and left in different directions. When they reached their car, they noticed a black Audi a few blocks away.

"Luke, didn't we see a black Audi at Sky Mountain?" Bobby commented.

"That's right we did, do you think they are following us?" Luke replied.

Both boys got in their car and pretended not to see the car. They drove a few blocks to see if the car began tailing them. As they pulled out onto the avenue, Bobby looked in his rear-view mirror and noticed the Audi slowly following them. They decided to speed up and see if the men in the car would keep up with them. Bobby thought of a few places to drive to and hide. He did not want to head back to the house for fear of them learning where they lived.

"Looks like those men are sticking with us." Bobby said excitedly.

"Can you lose them?" Luke replied.

"I have a few places in mind so hold on tight". Bobby gunned the engine and maneuvered in and out of traffic with expertise. Both boys had learned from their father proper evasive driving techniques from his time with the agency.

The Audi began to close in on the boys and Bobby knew

that this was going to be a close call. Suddenly the car was right on their bumper and Bobby looked at Luke with anticipation.

"Bobby, can you shake them?" Luke said worried.

"I'm trying." he replied.

Bobby jammed on the brakes causing the Audi to swerve from left to right. He turned the corner and sped down a side street with the Audi on their tail. Suddenly the car was right beside them and Bobby got a glimpse of the passenger's face. The man was middle aged and look to be of European descent. He jammed on the brakes again causing the Audi to speed by them and spin out.

Suddenly Luke's phone lit up and their high school pal Tony was face timing them. Luke answered the phone.

"Tony, you called at a bad time." Luke said sarcastically.

"Boys, where have you been, I've been looking for you." Tony said.

"We are little busy right now but, we have a lot to tell you." Bobby responded.

"You in trouble?" Tony replied worried.

"You could say that." Bobby joked.

"Tell us what we can do, and we are there." he said.

Luke brought Tony up to speed on all that had happened since yesterday. He told him to get the gang together and meet them at their house tonight. Tony agreed and said to let them know if they needed anything. The boys had good friends who had helped them on previous adventures.

Bobby raced down a few more side streets and turned right onto Fairfax Boulevard.

The Audi continued to be not far behind. Suddenly Bobby noticed the Audi had backed off and the boys had begun to distance themselves.

"Wonder what that was all about?" Luke said, eyeing the side mirror.

"Beats me but that was a close call for sure." Bobby replied.

On the way home the brothers tried to make some sense of all that had happened but came up with more questions than answers. As they got closer to home their thoughts shifted to what exactly was on that disc that they left with Mr. Peterson. Bobby wondered if leaving it there was such a good idea after all but felt sure that it would be in good hands.

It was after 2AM when both boys finally crashed into bed. Their friends had stayed up with them to discuss the latest mystery. All agreed they would talk more about it the next day when everyone had a good nights' sleep.

They arose next morning and discovered that an envelope had been left on the back seat of their car and they had not noticed it before. Luke anxiously opened the envelope and it was one sheet of Pioneer company letterhead with letters spelling out THE DISC OR DOOM.

Bobby looked at the letter that Luke had read, and they brought it into the kitchen.

"Sounds like these guys mean business." Luke said.

"They must have placed it there when we went to lunch." Bobby replied.

"We better be careful moving forward and keep this under wrap." Luke said.

"I agree and anxious to tell Dad all about what has happened" Bobby smiled.

The boys examined the note further and wanted to see if any fingerprints could be lifted from the paper. Bobby went to their father's study and grabbed the kit. As Bobby carefully applied the chemicals, he discovered that whoever it was that left the note was very careful not to leave any evidence.

"Just as I suspected, the person who left it was very careful." Bobby said.

"Well, this clue definitely opens more doors." Luke said hopefully.

"What do you mean?" Bobby questioned.

"Well, this is Pioneer letterhead, right? So now we know that somewhere there is access to company paper. Now we need to locate where it is." Luke said.

"But couldn't this person have just googled it and printed it out on regular paper?"

"No because this paper has special watermarks, see?" Luke said.

He showed Bobby the letterhead under the lamp and the Pioneer logo was visible.

Late that afternoon after running errands the boys pulled into the driveway and noticed their parents had arrived home from the vacation cruise. After entering the house, they were greeted by the warm embrace of their mother. She was a tall, attractive woman in her late forties who always worried about her inquisitive sons.

"Did you boys have fun while we were away?" Alice said with a smile.

"You could say that." Bobby said with a smile.

"Is Dad home?" Luke asked.

"Yes, he is upstairs in his study." Alice responded.

Both boys headed upstairs excitedly wanting to bring their father up to speed.

Upon entering their father's study, Bobby and Luke noticed their father going through files on his desk.

"Boys, come on in and have a seat." Mr. Robinson directed them to chairs.

The boys brought their father up to date on all that happened while they were away. They started by explaining the strange phone call and then the adventures near Sky

Mountain. They concluded their story by telling them they met with Mr. Peterson and the disc they found.

"How was the cruise, Dad?" Bobby asked.

"It was very relaxing, but I will say that I received an interesting text on my phone while we were sitting poolside on about the second day." He commented.

"What did it say?" Luke chimed in excitedly.

"All it said was Sky Mountain. It came from an unknown caller." their father replied.

Bobby shot a look at Luke and they both were thinking the same thing. This mystery was not just a coincidence. How did the person know their parents were on a cruise? How did they know their house phone number?

"Wait a second, wasn't your cruise near the Caymans?" Luke asked.

"Yes, this is what makes this mystery so intriguing." Mr. Robinson responded.

"How did they know," asked Luke, "you would be on a cruise, unless that person was as well."

"I was thinking that same thing." he responded. "What did the caller say when he called you boys?" Mr. Robinson inquired.

"The caller said Sky Mountain is the key to the puzzle." Luke recalled.

Luke remembered the note that was left on the backseat of their car and turned it over to their father. Mr. Robinson was a tall, handsome, lean figured man in his early fifties.

"We also discovered this on the back seat of the mustang." Bobby said.

Mr. Robinson took the note and placed it on his desk. He turned and began to search through his file cabinet for a file on Pioneer Corporation.

"There has to be some connection," said Bobby, "between

Sky Mountain and Pioneer Corporation and those men in the Audi. And who was flying the drone we heard overhead?"

Meanwhile Mr. Robinson was jotting down some notes on Pioneer.

"This may be connected to a new case I am working on," he said, "the two notes we received may be linked. I may need both of you boys on this next assignment."

Before he and Alice had left on their vacation, Mr. Robinson had met with Mr. Donald Pyles who was the CEO of a company called East Coast Mining Corp.

The company leases out heavy equipment for excavation projects. He had received a strange note from a Pioneer email account but could not figure out who had sent it.

"Who sent the company an email?" Bobby asked.

"That part is still unknown, and Mr. Pyles hired me to find out." He replied.

"So now we have two angles to approach," Bobby said, "and it's getting more and more complicated. Somebody is after these stolen plans for some reason."

"Well, what comes to mind first is Advanced Analytics." Luke said.

"But that would be too obvious." Mr. Robinson remarked.

Mr. Pyles had told Mr. Robinson that he was certain that there was something not right about this potential project. The company had been experiencing attempted break-ins to steal the equipment and each time had been stopped. Video surveillance via the Ring camera was unable to pick up any movements.

"Boys, I think we have two mysteries on our hands." Mr. Robinson smiled.

The next morning, Bobby and Luke met with their pals to discuss the latest updates on the new case they were involved with. Tony and Lee had been childhood friends and trusted confidantes. They all had assisted on previous cases and were up to the challenge. Soon, they were plotting who would get jobs at Advanced Analytics and East Coast Mining Corporation.

The Robinsons decided Tony and Lee would meet with Mr. Pyles who had arranged internships with their father. The boys would apply to get jobs at Advanced Analytics.

After a few days the applications were approved at Advanced Analytics and the boys were to start work the next Monday.

"Is it me or did it seem too easy to get jobs?" Bobby said perplexed.

"Well, they are growing company, but just the same, I agree." Luke replied.

"How do we want to play this?" Bobby asked.

Just then the doorbell rang, and it was their pals coming to give them the good news.

"We start next week, so what is the game plan?" Tony asked.

"I was just thinking the same thing on our end." Luke laughed.

Mr. Robinson had entered the room and was glad to see all the boys together.

After a long discussion on all that had happened up to this point, everyone agreed to be cautious moving forward.

"I think," Mr. Robinson answered, "that all of you boys working different angles to the mystery will be the only way it is solved – and working on the inside."

"Working as mailroom attendees," Bobby spoke up, "will allow both of us to snoop around without anyone getting suspicious of our being there."

Mr. Robinson did not know a lot about Advanced Analytics and cautioned the boys to be careful. All three agreed that the main objective of their jobs was to find out all they can about the company and at the same time see if there is any connection back to Pioneer Corporation.

The next day Mr. Peterson came by the house at the request of Mr. Robinson to discuss a game plan for the boys.

"Doug, come on in, it's great to see you". Both men shook hands

"Hi boys, I hear you got jobs in the mailroom." Mr. Peterson smiled.

"Yes, and it was surprisingly easy I must say." Bobby answered.

"You can thank my good friend Garrett Johnson for that", Doug answered, "I placed a call to him for his help. He was a Pioneer Corporation original in Human Resources but I wouldn't say he's loyal to Advanced."

"He was fond of Pioneer Corporation" Mr. Robinson chimed in.

"When Pioneer shut down after the CEO was killed, he knew something wasn't right and then when he knew it had to be plotted to destroy the company, it all made sense." Doug said.

The boys listened intently as Mr. Peterson detailed more of what happened to Pioneer Corporation. The company was very successful, but the belief was that someone had greed and wanted to make the company become their own.

"Wait, can we go back to this plane crash?" Luke asked.

"Yes, can you tell us more about what happened?" Bobby added.

Mr. Robinson explained that the CEO Avery Turnpike had taken a secret charter for a brief vacation down to the Cayman Islands. On board the flight also were his CFO Charles Goodwin and COO Allison Davis. On the return flight the plane suddenly developed engine trouble and crashed somewhere in the waters off Little Cayman. Search teams looked for the plane for five days but never found the plane.

"Wouldn't a flight plan have been filed?" Luke asked.

"Strangely there is no record of a return flight." Mr. Robinson replied.

"There has to be someone at the airport that would have witnessed the plane either taking off or landing in Grand Cayman or Dulles." Luke said.

"Avery was a good man," Doug said, "and had built the company from scratch. The technology they invented revolutionized the small aircraft industry. I don't know what happened to make the plane crash, but someone knows something, and I believe you boys can help."

"We will do all we can Mr. Peterson." Bobby said thoughtfully.

Mr. Peterson sat silent for a few moments, then his thoughts returned to the case.

"Ted, do you think the boys can pull this off as mail room attendants and be able to find out all about Advanced Analytics?" Doug asked.

"They look forward to the opportunity my friend." Mr. Robinson smiled.

"Well, here is the plan that Garrett and I had arranged, "he said looking at the boys, "Being employees in the mailroom will give them the opportunity to be all around the offices and no one will be suspicious."

Bobby and Luke looked on with great anticipation and the smiles on their faces couldn't hide this excitement.

"When did you say you boys were to start again?" Doug asked.

"We start on Monday." Luke replied. "The sooner the better."

"That's what I think as well." Doug replied.

"The boys will need to go online and learn all they can about the company in advance so let's get to work." Mr. Robinson announced.

"Maybe we can drive by the office this weekend." Tony responded.

"That's a great idea and we can learn the layout." Bobby said.

Mr. Robinson and Mr. Peterson told the boys they wanted to research further Pioneer Corporation and Advanced Analytics for possible employee connections as suspects.

"Hey fellas, how about we grab some dinner, and we can drive over to the office and check it out." Lee jumped in and spoke.

"Great idea, it's nice weather out so we can take the mustang," Luke responded.

The sun was setting on the warm summer night as the boys and their friends headed out to the restaurant. After talking over the plans at dinner they decided to drive by the Advanced Analytics office to get a layout. Upon entering the parking lot, the boys noticed a guard gate and decided to see if their names were added to the list.

As they pulled up, they noticed a disinterested guard eyeing them. Luke decided to play it cool and approached the gate house.

"The office is closed." said the rough looking guard.

"Yes, we know. We are starting on Monday and wanted to see if our names were added to the list. Bobby and Luke Robinson." Luke responded.

The guard eyed them suspiciously and went inside the check. He came back out and asked for their ID's. Luke handed them both.

"Your names are here and says you are working in the mailroom."

"Yes, we are interns arranged by Mr. Johnson." Luke said keeping his cool.

"We don't need any more people in the mailroom." The guard snapped.

"Well, that's nice of you to say but Mr. Johnson arranged it for us so we will listen to what he has to say." Bobby retorted.

The guard stared at the boys as they drove off. Still curious about the layout the group decided to try and find another way into the office parking lot and drove around the back side. They found a rear exit, but the gate was down and they left the property.

"What was his deal I wonder?" said Tony,

"And how did he know how many employees they need?" Luke chimed in

"Just the same, we will need to be careful on this one boy." Bobby said.

"On Monday, "said Luke, "we will need to play it cool and hopefully he won't be at the guard house, and we can make a good first impression."

CHAPTER 3

MAILROOM DETECTIVES

After reaching home, Tony and Lee said their goodbyes and got in their car. Luke and Bobby went into the house to discuss with their father the interaction with the unfriendly guard.

"He could just be doing his job seeing four teenagers." Mr. Robinson smiled.

"Well, he was a serious grouch." Bobby laughed.

Mr. Robinson sat with the boys, and they went over some files he found on Pioneer Corporation. As they scanned through news reports they had more questions now than answers.

"We need to find out what happened to the plane." Luke spoke up.

"First things first son, we need to start from the beginning of the end of Pioneer Corporation and what caused them to shut their doors." Mr. Robinson said.

"You're right Dad, where do we start?" Luke replied.

"Do we know any former employees who could shine a light on this?" Bobby asked.

"There might be one person who could help." Mr. Robinson said.

"Who's that?" Bobby asked.

"A person by the name of Gilbert Sullivan." Mr. Robinson said. "He retired about six months before they closed their doors. I don't think he had anything to do with it, maybe even wasn't aware of what truly happened. But he did work in the accounting office so he would have had access to financial records."

"Where can we find him?" Luke asked.

"He lives in the mountains near Culpepper on a farm." Mr. Robinson replied.

"How do you know him, Dad?" Bobby asked.

"I have known Gilbert for many years. He was helpful in a case we had about 10 years ago, and we stayed in touch. He's a good man. When he noticed some financial discrepancies, he went to Avery and Charles. They asked who could help and he mentioned my name." Mr. Robinson said. He continued with the story of how the executives became alarmed by some missing documents and started an investigation.

"And that's when they went to the Caymans?" Luke asked.

"Precisely son. They had offshore accounts and wanted to confirm privately that what they had was exactly as it should be." Mr. Robinson replied. "After the plane was lost, suddenly the company was losing clients and funds and eventually had to lay off employees and close their doors."

"I can't wait to get started on Monday." Luke said excitedly.

"Garrett Johnson will meet you on Monday and begin the process to have you go to work in the mailroom." Mr. Robinson said. "Remember boys, he is the only one who knows your true reason for being there, so be careful."

"We will Dad, you can count on it." Bobby said smiling.

The boys enjoyed a relaxing Sunday getting ready for the next day's work assignment. They studied Advance Analytics a little more online and brought themselves up to speed on news articles.

Monday morning arrived and they promptly arrived at the guard gate at 9am. The same guard they had encountered the other night was not on duty and that was a relief to the boys to get started on the right foot.

"Bobby and Luke, welcome to Advanced Analytics." said Garrett as they entered his office and shook hands warmly. The boys could tell by the look in Garrett's eyes that it would be a good assignment and that he wanted to find out what really happened.

"Thanks for hiring us, this is going to be perfect for our college courses." Bobby said.

"Yes, being undergrads for our software engineering degrees this will help us tremendously." Luke piled on.

After getting their company ID's printed up and all the paperwork filled out, Garrett walked them back to the mailroom and introduced them to their new boss.

"Boys, this is Gus Wolanski, he will be your boss." Garrett said.

Gus was a bald, heavyset man in his mid-thirties with bushy eyebrows. His demeanor reminded the boys of their high school coach who was rough around the edges.

"Gus, I would like you to meet your new mailroom attendees, Luke and Bobby Robinson." Garrett said politely.

"We have enough people to handle the job" Gus replied, appearing to be annoyed with new employees.

"We need more people to handle the mail, and this was approved by upper management." Garrett replied firmly.

"Well, I guess there is nothing I can do about it but step

out of line and you both won't be here long". Gus said and walked away grumbling to himself.

"What a swell guy." Luke said jokingly to Bobby with his hand on his hips.

"Just the same, let's keep on our toes with him." Bobby cautioned.

"Got it." Luke replied.

Both boys reported to the mailroom to begin their rounds of delivering the mail to assigned offices in the building. With their new boss eyeing them the boys maintained silence while sorting the mail.

Suddenly Bobby noticed one piece of mail that was addressed to Mr. A. Turnpike. He turned to his brother and very nonchalantly showed him the letter under the table.

Luke slowly glanced at the letter without drawing any attention to himself and gave his brother a raised eyebrow look. Bobby looked around and noticed their boss was looking at a piece of equipment and he quickly put the envelope back in the pile with the rest.

Later, while the boys were at lunch, they discussed the letter.

"That sure was strange to see a letter for Avery." Luke commented.

"It sure was, but I'm wondering if he really did die in the plane crash." Bobby said.

He continued with his thoughts, "I mean they never did find the plane. Maybe he was faking his death."

"We can never rule anything out, but it's strange we came across it." Luke replied.

"Agreed, it had this address and an office number." Bobby responded.

The boys made their rounds to the assigned offices to deliver the mail. One floor had only three offices. Upon entering an office with the name Rota-Vonni & Associates the boys became more suspicious.

"What's wrong?" Luke asked Bobby.

"This is the office for A. Turnpike." Bobby replied, showing him the letter.

"That sure is strange." Luke said.

They looked around the office and could not find anyone to deliver the mail to, so they set it down on the main desk. As they were walking out the door, Bobby noticed in one of the offices a picture of Avery Turnpike beside the plane he had chartered.

Just then the office manager returned, and the boys made their way out the door.

"That's spooky to see that picture of Avery Turnpike in that office." said Bobby.

"Are you thinking what I'm thinking?" Luke shot back.

"Yep, and I never believed in ghosts before", said Bobby in frightened voice, "But I may be changing my mind since I saw that picture."

Bobby and Luke, spooked by the picture in the office, made their way to the other offices to finish the rounds.

"There has to be some explanation for that office and Mr. Turnpike."

Bobby said.

"Yeah, but what could it be?" Luke replied. "We could look up that company when we get home and investigate it more."

"Agreed." Bobby said.

As the boys were getting close to the elevator, the doors swung open and discovered Garrett was standing there.

"Hey fellas, how's the first day going?" Garrett asked.

"We are delivering the mail like we are supposed to." Luke smiled.

"That's great." Garrett said patting Luke on the back. "Say, I have an assignment for the both of you." Garrett showed them some papers that showed a new company moving into the building and would need an escort to their new office.

"We'd be happy to. What time are they getting here?" Bobby asked.

"Should be arriving within the hour so head on up to the 5th floor and wait for them there. I'll tell Gus what you are doing." Garrett shook hands and walked back to the elevator.

Bobby and Luke finished their rounds and headed up to the 5th floor to wait for this new company. They continued to discuss what happened at the mysterious office of Rota-Vonni & Associates.

Luke got out his cell phone to text their father what had happened.

"The cell coverage in this building isn't the greatest." Luke moaned.

"You would figure with all these tech companies it would be better, and more reliable." Bobby replied.

"My text won't go through; I'll try when we are done." Luke said dejected.

The boys waited around the office for about 30 minutes for the new company to arrive.

"What's taking them so long?" Bobby asked.

"I don't know, but let's give it another 30 minutes and then we can go back down to the mailroom." Luke replied.

Suddenly the elevator chimed, and the doors opened to see two men with large pieces of furniture. They turned off the elevator and began to unload the items.

"Thought you guys would never show up." Luke joked.

One of the men was clearly not in a joking mood and began to unload the furniture. He was a thin, wiry looking man in his early twenties. His partner looked to be about the same age.

"We were delayed downstairs." he commented.

"We'll give you a hand in unloading." Bobby said.

It took about an hour for all the men to unload the furniture and filing cabinets in the new office. The boys tried to make small talk with the men, but it was no use.

They appeared to be agitated that they were getting help to set up the office. As Luke and Bobby helped to place the office furniture, they noticed the men had disappeared. Suddenly the office door locked, and the boys could not get out.

"Hey, open the door." Luke yelled.

From underneath the door they noticed what appeared to be a heavy fog drifting into the office.

"Smoke!" Bobby yelled.

"That's not smoke, that's sleeping gas that's coming in." Luke replied as they both frantically searched for any towels to jam against the bottom of the door. Both boys were now in panic mode as to how to escape. They tried the door again with no luck. The windows in the office were just glass panels that could not open from the inside. They began to cough and tried to muffle the smell with their Tee shirts. Soon they blacked out.

The boys awoke to find themselves in an empty office. They were sitting on the floor in the middle of the room. Blindfolded with their hands tied, they wriggled out and took off their masks.

"You okay?" Bobby asked Luke as he untied his ankles.

"I feel embarrassed we fell into that trap." Luke responded.

The young detectives made their way to the elevator to report what had happened to them when they realized they were not on the 5th floor.

"Wait a second!" Luke announced.

"For what?" Bobby announced.

"This says we are on the 6th floor," Luke pointed to the sign above the elevator, "But I know for a fact we were helping those men on the 5th floor. Let's get back down there and see what is going on." Luke replied angrily.

"You're right." Bobby said noticing the elevator sign.

The boys arrived on the 5th floor and headed for the office where they had helped to arrange the furniture.

They opened the main office door and found everything in its place as they had left it, but no sign of the two men. Bobby and Luke were now convinced that something strange was going on in this office.

Gus appeared at the doorway with Garrett right behind him.

"Where have you both been?" Gus asked firmly.

"We were held hostage and sleeping gas was filtered under the door." Luke responded, trying to keep his cool.

"That's nonsense." Gus shot back.

"It's true, we were helping those men that Garrett asked us to help move in and arrange office furniture on the 5th floor." Bobby replied.

"Garrett, is this true, are they telling the truth?" Gus asked.

"I did ask them to help, but where did they go?" Garrett remarked.

"That's what we came back to find out." Luke said.

All four of the men headed down the office hallway. Upon entering one office, they noticed a group of people beginning to set up desks and phones. Neither of the boys recognized anyone in the office and began to wonder who those other two men were.

"Excuse me, "Bobby announced, "but do you have two other men who are helping you move in today?"

"I'm sorry no, this is the whole team." replied a tall, thin woman who appeared to be in her early forties.

"You have us mistaken for another office." Another man replied.

"No, this is the right office." Luke replied firmly.

"What is the name of your company?" Bobby inquired.

"I'm sorry to be rude, but we have work to do." A short, heavyset man replied in response to Bobby's question.

"It's a simple question." Bobby retorted.

"If you must know," said the thin woman, "we are an accounting firm called Anderson CPA. Now, please leave us to finish."

"Let's go boys and let them finish". Garrett said nervously.

The four left the office and walked back to the elevator and discussed all that had happened to the Robinson boys.

"What do you make of all this Luke?" Bobby asked.

"That's two strange companies now, are we thinking too much into it?"

"I don't think so, but let's keep our eyes and ears open." Bobby said.

"You two need to get back to work and finish your rounds." Gus replied.

The Robinson's continued their assigned rounds the next few days cautious to keep their eyes open to any more suspicious activity. They decided they would meet up with their friends at home before dinner on Friday to discuss the week's activities. When they left the building on Friday they went out to their car and noticed the two men waiting there for them in another car. The men drove up slowly and rolled down the window.

"If you know what's good for you," said the passenger who had long bushy hair and a tattoo of a bulldog on his right arm. "You'll stop snooping around the office."

"We weren't snooping pal!" Luke shot back.

"We didn't ask for any help unloading". The man said angrily.

The men proceeded to gun the engine and raced off and disappeared around the corner out of sight before Bobby could respond if they were the ones who put sleeping gas under the door.

The boys got in their car and Luke texted Lee to meet them at Outback Steakhouse around 6:00pm.

"What do you make of those people in the office the other day?" Bobby asked his brother.

"Our questions sure made them uneasy seeing as how they had no idea who we were, but they were trying to cover up something for sure."

The young detectives decided to go back to the building to snoop around and since they had their ID's on them, would not draw any suspicions.

"Where should we start first?" Bobby asked his brother.

"Let's start at the top floor and work our way down." Luke replied.

"Good idea, but let's keep a low profile and stay away from the lobby."

They agreed to do a search and if they were stopped, especially by Gus, would plead their innocence and say they forgot to put the mail cart back as cover. They went up in the service elevator and got off at the 7th floor.

Walking down the hallways they peered into the offices looking for any clues as to where those two men were employed As they worked their way down to the 6th floor suddenly Bobby sensed they were being watched. He glanced behind him, and a building security guard approached them.

"Are you boys finished for the day?" the guard asked.

"We forgot where we placed the mail cart," Bobby replied,

feigning innocence. "This is a summer job and we just started." He nudged Luke to agree.

"Should we not be in the office now?", Bobby asked. "Are we in some kind of trouble?"

"The security officer in the lobby received a call about two suspicious individuals walking around in the building, so we had to check it out." the guard explained.

"I wonder who made the call?" Luke spoke up.

"We don't know, it was an anonymous caller." the guard replied.

Bobby looked at Luke and they apologized to the guard and said they would head out now.

"No harm done fellows, it's your first week." He smiled and walked away. The young detectives made their way out of the building and headed to their car. Luke looked up and could see two men peering out of a 5th floor window.

"Bobby, look up there!" Luke said, pointing upwards.

"Those aren't the two men who tied us up!" Bobby shot back.

"How come we couldn't find them before?" Luke said angrily.

"I don't know," he answered, "but I'm determined to find out what is really going on in that office".

"What do you suggest?" Luke asked excitedly.

"I think we will come back tonight and scope it out. We may stumble across a great clue. I just have that funny feeling." Bobby smiled.

"Good call let's meet the fellows. Wait a second! What if our friendly guard is on duty tonight?" Luke proposed.

"You're right. Well, maybe we park in the area where we can see the 5th floor from a better vantage point." he said before dinner.

All four boys met up at the Robinson house to discuss

the latest adventures with their father and a plan of action for later that evening. Bobby and Luke were anxious to know who those two other men were in the window this afternoon. Mr. Robinson sat in on the conversation listening to the boys and then spoke up.

"Boys, I believe you are on the right track, just be careful". He warned.

"We will Dad." Luke promised.

The young detectives and their friends headed to a quick dinner and then to scout out locations where they could get a good vantage point on the building. They were sure that something was going to happen tonight. They parked around the corner with a good view of the 5th floor.

"Should we go in for a closer look?" Luke asked.

"Lee and I will get out and try to get up closer, "Bobby replied. "You and Tony stay here and have your phones ready to get a photo if you spot something."

The boys got out and proceeded to work their way quickly and quietly towards the building. They noticed a coffee shop that had a good view and would be a perfect cover if they needed to act fast.

As Bobby quietly moved in the direction of the office he happened to glance up and noticed a figure in the window. When he motioned to Lee to look up and glanced back it was gone.

"Did you see that?" He whispered.

"No, I missed it." Lee replied.

CHAPTER 4

SIGNALS AT MIDNIGHT

Suddenly two figures reappeared in the window. Bobby could not make out what they were trying to do. He called out to Luke.

"Luke, do you see those men?" He asked.

"I sure do, but I think I'm too far away to get a picture". Luke replied.

The next moment all four boys noticed that the figures were using a laser pointer out the window in some form of signal. Bobby rushed closer to the guard house and noticed no one was there. In a blinding flash, he saw the lights of a van pulling into the parking lot. *No one was at the wheel.*

"There's no one driving the van!" Bobby warned Lee.

"What do you mean, there has to be!" Lee shot back.

"It makes no sense I know." Bobby replied.

The van continued through the gates and made a left turn into the parking garage. Both boys followed in pursuit but then the garage doors closed. Luke and Tony arrived, and all four boys debated their next steps.

"Did anyone get the license plate number?" Luke asked.

"I think I did." Bobby checked the pictures on his phone and even though the shot was blurry he expanded it. "Here it is, it's a local tag and looks to be a rental."

"What could they be bringing in at this late hour?" Tony asked.

"You guys have your badges; can't you get us in?" Lee said.

"Let's go." Bobby said excitedly.

The boys made their way quickly and quietly around to the side of the building and headed to the employee entrance.

"Wait, I just thought of something". Bobby said, stopping the group in their tracks.

"What is it?" Luke replied.

"The entrance will have a camera and we will be spotted. What excuse would we provide? And what if the security guard is in cahoots with those men on the fifth floor?" Bobby asked.

"That's a good point, didn't think of that." Luke grinned.

"I got it!" Bobby announced. "Tony, since they won't recognize you and Lee, go the main entrance. Since they won't know you two, you can pretend your car broke down and you need to make a call to a towing company. This will turn their attention away from the monitor."

"Good call, we're on it." Tony replied.

Tony and Lee headed out and went to the main entrance. The group decided to use text communications to maintain silence. As the boys approached the main entrance, they could see a guard sitting at the desk inside.

"Here we go, let's make it a good one." Tony fist-bumped Lee.

They entered the round swinging doors and approached the main desk. A burly looking man in his early thirties was positioned at the desk looking at some papers. He looked up and gave an expression of annoyance.

"Can I help you gentlemen?" He said in a monotone voice.

"Yes, our car stalled out on us," Tony replied acting, "and we were wondering if we could make a call to get a tow truck to help?"

"What's wrong with your cellphone in your hand?" he replied not buying what the boys were trying to sell.

"The coverage isn't great in this area." Lee spoke up in defense.

The guard eyed them both for a few seconds and then looked at his monitors. He turned to make a phone call and as he did Tony quietly and quickly texted the thumbs up emoji code to Bobby on his phone. Earlier the group had decided that using this could quickly alert others instead of texting out a message.

"We're in, run for it!" Bobby whispered to Luke when his phone lit up from Tony.

Both boys made a beeline for the employee entrance. Using a key code password, they opened the door and looked for a quick hiding place. They scanned the area for the security cameras and happened to notice one in the corner aimed at the employee entrance.

They immediately ran for cover and hid behind boxes by the door leading to the service elevator. They texted Tony a thumbs up emoji.

"Your tow truck should be here in ten minutes." The guard said looking back at the boys.

"Thanks, we will wait out front." Tony replied. He had silenced his phone so he could not immediately check his phone to see if Bobby and Luke had made it in. When they got outside, he looked at his phone and noticed Bobby had responded. He felt a wave of relief and both boys went around the corner and hid near the employee entrance to wait for more news from their friends.

"Where do we go from here?" Luke asked his brother.

"Let's try the stairwell but keep an eye out for cameras," he replied.

After texting Lee to keep his eyes open and respond to them any unusual goings-on around the employee entrance, the brothers headed for the fifth floor. Both were quiet, pondering over all that had happened in the last twenty-four hours. *Who had signaled the red beam? Was there more action planned for tonight with a signal call?* This case, both boys agreed, was becoming more and more puzzling.

They quickly and quietly worked their way up the stairs looking all around for any cameras in the stairwell. They reached the fifth-floor door and listened for any noises.

"What should we do now?" Luke asked anxiously.

"If we open this door they could be right there." Bobby answered.

They listened some more and in barely an audible tone they heard two men arguing across the hall.

"Are you sure they know where to land?" a voice echoed.

"Yes, dammit, they do but I can't keep signaling or someone will notice we are up here," another man responded sternly. "The guard at the desk told me he would alert us if anyone came by."

The man with the deep voice called down to the desk to check in.

"Has anyone come by?" He asked.

He hung up the phone and told the other man that only two bratty kids came by looking for a tow truck. Bobby and Luke looked at each other and smiled knowing their plan was working.

A phone rang and one of the men answered it.

"We will be ready, make sure you go around back and use the loading dock. We will be right there." The voice replied. "Only Frank and I are here, Donte is at the main desk keeping an eye on cameras."

"Ask him which office we should get the stuff out of." The second man replied.

Bobby looked at Luke with an expression of surprise.

"What office could they be talking about?" Bobby whispered.

Both boys heard the elevator chime and doors opening and closing indicating the men had gotten on the elevator. Now was their chance to snoop around and see what all the action was about. Bobby opened the door quietly and looked in both directions. The crept along the hallway towards the elevator keeping their eyes and ears peeled for any other men that might be on the floor. As they neared the corner Bobby noticed out of the corner of his eye a camera was placed hanging from the ceiling aimed at the elevator. He motioned his brother back.

"I see a camera aimed at the elevator". Bobby alerted Luke.

"What should we do?" he asked quizzically.

"Let's head back to the area they were at and go into the office to look for more clues". He replied.

Bobby and Luke walked back to the area by the stairwell door and opened the office door directly across the hall. They gasped at what they saw spread throughout the room.

"These are all the Pioneer boxes!" Bobby said with a shocked look on his face.

"How in the world did these get up here?" Luke asked.

"I don't know but this proves my theory that somebody sabotaged Pioneer and is starting a new company."

"But there is no way to get rid of these boxes before those men decide to come back." Luke warned.

"My thoughts exactly." Bobby shot back.

"Let's take one quickly and hide it in the janitorial closet down the hallway for safe keeping just to have proof." Bobby had suggested.

"Won't they notice one is missing?" Luke responded.

"I doubt it, they aren't marked," he said.

"Let's take a quick video and photos to prove these are here and what floor and office they are currently in?" Luke proposed.

"Good idea". Bobby replied. He got out his phone and did a slow pan around the room and took about twenty quick photos. Luke picked up a box and quickly ran down the hallway and stored it in a closet and made sure to lock the door. Bobby then sent the video and photos to Tony to let him in on what's going on.

Suddenly the boys heard the elevator chime and quickly looked out the office door to see the floor lights moving.

"Hide." Bobby warned him.

Both boys made a quick run to the office next door which was vacant but not before noticing on a table next to the door a pair of flight tickets. Bobby quickly took a photo of it before dashing out the door. They hid in a closet in the office and put their ears to the wall to listen in on the conversations.

"Donte has assured us no one is at the loading dock, "one of the men said as they walked into the office next door. "Let's get these on the dolly and start heading downstairs."

The men quickly loaded up the boxes making sure to be as quiet as possible. Periodically one of the men would peer out the door to see if anyone was in the hallway. After securing the boxes, they slowly rolled them down the hallway towards the elevator.

"What time is our flight out of Dulles to the Caymans?" The other man said.

The other man pulled out his phone and looked up the flight time.

"11:30am but I have been told we will have no problems."

Bobby looked at Luke and now knew where the two men and illegal goods were headed. They heard the men load up the last boxes and move down the hallway towards the elevator. After hearing no more sounds the boys came out of their hiding place and quietly peeked out the door.

"I think the coast is clear." Bobby said.

"Let's grab that box out of the janitor closet and see what's in it." Luke replied, as he walked back to the closet.

"How will we get it out of here?" Bobby said. "That guard is still at the desk."

"He can't be the real guard if he is working with those guys, can he?" Luke asked.

"My hunch is no and that the real guard is tied up somewhere in the building. Remember we haven't met everybody here," Bobby said. "We must find him and then somehow get on that plane those men are getting on tomorrow."

The boys grabbed the box and went into the empty office. They searched for any clues the men might have left behind. Bobby texted Tony to let them know what was happening. He asked him to sneak around the front and see if the guard was still sitting at the front desk.

Bobby opened the box and peered inside. He and Luke noticed a bunch of old Pioneer Corporation files.

"Why would they want papers from a company that no longer exists? Bobby questioned.

"It all goes back to when we found that safe near Sky Mountain." Luke added.

"The big question is where they are taking those boxes and how many did they take?" Bobby replied.

"Let's get this out of here." Luke said.

Suddenly Bobby's phone started ringing and he reached into his pocket and quickly answered it.

"Is the guard still there?" Bobby asked.

"No and Lee went around to the loading dock to see if he could get a better look at what's going on." Tony replied.

"I knew it." Luke said.

"I just thought of something," Bobby said. "This is Friday which means they planned this whole thing perfectly. No one will be around over the weekend."

"What should we do Bobby?" Tony asked.

"Text Lee and we will meet you outside back behind the dumpsters so we can look straight at the loading dock. If you can, get a photo of the truck's license plate." he said.

"Got it." Tony said and hung up.

"Let's take this to our car and then meet them." Bobby said.

Luke grabbed the box of papers and they quickly headed down the side stairs and out to their car where they placed the box in their trunk. Then, they headed back to meet the others behind the dumpster.

"Did you get a photo of the license?" Bobby asked.

"Definitely." Tony replied.

CHAPTER 5

DANGEROUS CROSSING

The boys hid behind some boxes and watched as the men loaded boxes into the van. One by one they loaded close to thirty white boxes and closed the back of the van.

"Drive to the airport and the crew will meet you there." One of the men said to another.

Bobby whispered to Luke. "We must get tickets to the Caymans."

"What if they spot us?" Luke responded with fear.

"We can't let them get away, no matter how dangerous it is. We must see where this potential danger takes us." Bobby smiled.

After discussing the plan with their father, quickly packing and arranging for flights, the boys headed to the airport the next day to Grand Cayman. As they approached the ticket counter, they spotted Gus at the next counter.

"What's he doing here?" Luke wondered.

"We can't have him spot us; it will blow our cover." Bobby warned. Just then, they noticed Gus looking in their direction.

The boys quickly turned to look in the other direction. With nervous energy they turned back and spoke with the ticket agent.

"Here are your boarding passes, "said the blonde woman who appeared to be in her early twenties. "Your flight will leave out of Gate 25. Have a safe trip."

"Thanks." The boys said in unison.

The young detectives picked up their bags and discussed the best way to get to the gate while at the same time keeping an eye out if they spotted Gus again. When they looked over at the next counter he was no longer there.

"That was a close call." Luke said wiping his forehead.

"I'll say, maybe he didn't notice it was us at first." Bobby replied.

"Where are our seats again?" Luke asked looking at his boarding pass.

"Row 29, seats A and C." Bobby replied.

"Well, what do we do if he is on the same flight?" Luke said.

"We just make up a story that we are going to see friends and act like it's just a coincidence." Bobby said.

The boys made their way through the airport to Gate 25 on time. They did not come across Gus at all and began to wonder if he was even on their flight and if they had worried unnecessarily?

The ticket agent began the pre-flight boarding process and rows were called. Suddenly they noticed Gus approaching the seating area. Since they were in one of the back rows they would board first, and he might not notice them at all. Gus sat down and opened his laptop and was oblivious to those around him.

"Now boarding rows 25-30, please step forward." The agent called out. The boys gathered their bags and headed to the counter. Gus did not move and that brought a sigh of relief to the detectives.

The detectives made their way to the rear of the plane and stowed their bags in the overhead compartment. They settled in the seats and kept a lookout for Gus. A few minutes went by and no sign of their co-worker.

"Luke, look at who's working his way down the aisle." Bobby nudged his brother.

"Keep your head down so he doesn't notice us." Luke warned.

Gus put his bag in the overhead compartment and motioned to his partner to do the same.

"Who's he traveling with I wonder?" Bobby said quizzically.

"Beats me." Luke replied.

The men collected themselves and sat down in their seats and began chatting with each other. The boys could not hear what was being said. The other man got up and made his way to the rear to use the restroom. As he passed the boys they pretended to be in deep conversation. They did not recognize who it was but then Bobby had a chilling thought. *What if Gus comes to use the restroom while on the flight? He will for sure recognize them.*

"Our best bet is to act cool". Bobby told Luke.

"We just happened to be on the same flight". Luke responded.

"Right." Bobby agreed. "And thank goodness Dad was able to secure hotel reservations at the Grand Caymanian Resort since he knows the General Manager."

"What's the plan once we get there?" Luke asked.

"Our first plan is to find out where they are going to be

staying. We can rent a jeep and get around George Town easily. Most hotels are on Seven Mile Beach." Bobby said.

The man returned to his seat from the bathroom and didn't appear to recognize the boys. Now the plan was to just keep an eye on them the whole flight to the Caymans.

The flight was uneventful all the way to Grand Cayman. The plane touched down at Owen Roberts International Airport. The boys disembarked with the other passengers and worked their way through customs. They approached the baggage claim area and picked up their luggage. They spotted Gus and the other man getting their bags as well. Gus was on the phone walking around nervously. The boys made their way to the rental car desk to pick up their vehicle.

Luke spotted the men getting on a bus for the Marriott. This was a good sign. Now they knew where the men were staying.

"Got the jeep, let's head out." Bobby said.

"They headed on the bus to the Marriott." Luke pointed out.

"Good, let's follow that bus and we can check into our hotel later. "Bobby said enthusiastically.

The boys followed the Marriott bus as it made its way from the airport through George Town.

After a few stops, the men got off at the full-service Marriott. Bobby parked the jeep in the parking lot and they worked their way to the main lobby. They sat in deep cushioned chairs and surveyed the area. Both men checked into their rooms and made their way to the elevator.

"Should we wait around to see if they come back down and head out?" Luke asked.

"Let's give it thirty minutes and see what they do." Bobby responded. "They didn't rent any vehicle, so no matter what they do they have to catch an Uber."

"Good point." Luke shot back.

After waiting the set time and not seeing the men return to the lobby the boys gave up and decided to head to their hotel and check in and get settled. They returned to their jeep and noticed one of the tires were flat.

"Just great, how did that happen?" Bobby said frustrated.

"We must have run over a nail." Luke said surprised.

Suddenly the boys were startled to see a light blue van fast approaching them. They made a frantic leap out of the way just in time. The van just narrowly missed hitting them and crashing into their jeep.

"That was close!" Luke exclaimed.

Bobby got up and dusted off his clothes. "Someone did that on purpose!" He said angrily.

"It couldn't be those men; they didn't have a car." Luke said, also dusting off his clothes.

The van came to a stop sign and had to wait for traffic to ease. Both boys chased after the van and got up close to the driver's side. Bobby banged on the window. The frightened man rolled down his window and peered at Bobby with a look of horror.

"What's the big idea?" Bobby said angrily.

The man who appeared to be in his late sixties with white hair looked at Bobby with fright.

"I'm so sorry, are you alright young man?" The man whimpered.

"Luckily, yes, but you almost hit my brother and I." he said.

The passenger rolled down his window and looked at Luke.

"Didn't you see us standing by our jeep?" Luke asked.

"I looked away for just a moment. Two men approached us and wanted to pay us for our van.

They were insistent and I said no, and we just got out of there as fast as we could." He replied.

"What men?" Luke asked, guessing who it was.

"Two large men, one was bald and appeared to be about thirty."

"Gus!" Both boys said in unison.

"Do you know them?" The man said surprised.

"Yes, we do, but it's not of any concern for you." Bobby said.

"I'm just glad you boys are alright." The man said.

The boys shook hands and headed back to their jeep.

"Well, they know we are here, so no surprise now." Luke said shrugging his shoulders.

"This just means we have to be careful now." Bobby urged.

"Agreed." Luke responded.

"But how did they know we followed them," Bobby wondered.

"We didn't take the same bus and followed in the jeep. There's no way they knew that was us."

"Maybe that man on the flight knew us, or Gus saw us in the baggage area." Luke said thoughtfully.

"But still, they can't see out of the back of the bus to know it was us that was following them. It had to be after they checked in and during the time, we waited for them that they spotted us sitting in the lobby." Bobby wondered.

Exhausted from their long trip, the young detectives checked into their hotel on West Bay. With a wonderful view of the bay, the boys sat on their balcony to discuss their next steps. They facetimed to their father to bring him up to speed.

"You boys be careful; it sounds like Gus and his friend already know you are there and will be trailing them." Their father said.

"Where should we go from here?" Luke asked.

"Go see Darren at a company called Dive Tek," he said. "He may be able to shed some light on any crashes that may have happened there. He's a son of my one former agents."

"By the way, what is your excuse for not going to work the next couple of days?" He asked.

"We didn't think about that part of it." Luke confessed.

"I'll take care of it on my end, just be careful." Their father promised.

"Thanks Dad." Bobby said. They signed off and discussed the case a little more as they took the jeep out and drove to the East End of the island.

The next morning, the boys rose for an early breakfast in the restaurant. They were eager to start their sleuthing and would stop in at Dive Tek as they promised their father. Dressed in light shirts and shorts to bear the Caribbean heat, the detectives hopped in their jeep and headed up W Bay Road and merged with NW Point Rd till they saw the sign for Dive Tek. They got out of the jeep and made their way to the entrance.

"Excuse me, but we are looking for Darren?" Bobby asked the young woman seated behind the desk.

"May I ask who is calling?" She replied.

"We are sons of Ted Robinson. He gave us Darren's name as a point of contact."

"Just a moment." She went back into the back office and came out a few minutes later with a man who appeared to be in his late twenties with bleach blonde hair and a deep tan.

"Hi fellas, I'm Darren, how can I help you?" he said cordially.

"My name is Bobby, and this is my brother Luke," he said as they shook hands. "Our father Ted Robinson said you might be able to help us in tracking down a private jet that crashed off Grand Cayman a few years back."

He sat down at the desk and thought for a moment. He finally said, "I do remember something about that. I had just started here, and it happened under mysterious circumstances."

"Our understanding," Luke chimed in, "is that this plane was never found. Is that true?"

"There are so many wrecks in the Caribbean and the currents can get strong." Darren replied.

"What type of plane was it again?" Darren asked as he turned to look through his filing cabinet.

"We believe it was a Piper PA-23 Apache." Luke responded.

Darren searched through his files and came across one that was dated 2018. He flipped through the pages and noticed one that had a newspaper article clipped to it. It read, *Plane carrying CEO disappears*. He turned back to the detectives.

"Here it is, I found it." He said handing the article to Bobby.

Bobby showed it to Luke and began to read the headline.

"A charter plane carrying the CEO of Pioneer Corporation crashed off the coast of the Cayman Islands," Bobby began to read. "Search crews spanned the area for five days but were unable to find the aircraft. The National Transportation Safety Board, known as the NTSB, contracted with a local dive company to assist in the search for the plane. The last known communication was near the outer islands known as Little Cayman and Cayman Brac. After a lengthy search, crews were called off and the mystery remains."

"Wow, so they never really did find it." Bobby exclaimed.

"Nope, and our crews weren't asked to continue." Darren replied.

"Where are these other islands exactly?" Luke inquired.

Darren showed the boys a map on the wall of all three

islands and their exact position on the big map of Grand Cayman. He showed them the mark on the map just between Little Cayman and Cayman Brac where the last known contact from the plane occurred.

"And you said currents are strong here in the Caymans?" Bobby asked.

"Yes, generally in the months of August and September," he said,

"Hurricanes can churn the waters and make it choppy. I believe the Plane did go down in late August if I remember correctly. This would explain why it would have been so hard to find. Now this being close to four years ago, who knows where it could be now."

"I agree, this would make tracking it down near impossible, but Luke and I would like to give it a try." Bobby said.

"Yes, we have our diving certifications." Luke chimed in.

"Let me check with the president of the company and get his approval."

Darren said, then proceeded to go to the office. After about fifteen minutes, he returned.

"All the charters today are full, but we can schedule one for mid-afternoon tomorrow, would that work?" Darren said.

Both boys were not surprised that the charters were sold out and decided to take him up on his offer.

"Tomorrow works for us. Do we fill out the papers now or do that in the morning?" Bobby inquired.

"We can take care of that now." Darren replied. He went to the filing cabinet and handed the boys the waiver forms and the payment information. After about an hour of solidifying the excursion, the boys thanked Darren and headed out.

The young detectives decided to check out some of the tourist attractions on the island and drove around in their jeep. They noted on their map a little town not too far away called Hell.

Hell is an area within the district of West Bay, Grand Cayman. Its name comes from a group of short, black, limestone formations located in the area. It's eerie with a rather sinister look is what gave it its infamous name. Visitors are not permitted to walk on the limestone formations but viewing platforms are provided. A gift shop and service station are in the area, and art depicting Satan can be seen when entering.

Bobby and Luke checked out the area and mailed a few postcards to family and friends back home.

"Wait till they see where this is post marked from." Luke laughed.

"Kind of creepy if you ask me." Bobby smiled.

They drove all around the island, which is only seventy-six square miles. The sun was bright and beating down and they got to work on their tan.

"Let's check out one of the restaurants for dinner tonight and see what they offer." Bobby suggested.

"Sounds good to me." Luke replied.

The young detectives went back to their hotel room to relax before heading out to dinner. They inquired at the front desk about good local restaurants. The concierge recommended a restaurant called The Grand Wharf, which is in the shopping district of George Town.

After placing a call and reserving two seats for seven o'clock, the boys headed out in their jeep. The sun set in the western sky like fresh colors brushed upon an artist's canvas. The glow of lights shone bright upon the shops that lined both sides of the street.

Bobby parked the jeep in the parking lot and the boys made their way into the restaurant. They were seated along the water with a breathtaking view of the ocean and the large cruise ships that were stationed off the coast.

"We should bring the girls here, "Bobby said, "they would love this view." Both boys had long-term steady girlfriends from high school who they regularly dated.

"I agree." Luke replied.

At nine o'clock a bell rang out signifying the nightly ritual of the restaurant chef bringing a bucket of fish to feed the Tarpon swimming in the water as the crowds got up from their tables to witness the extraordinary event.

CHAPTER 6

TROUBLE BELOW

The event thrilled everyone young and old and is one of the main draws to the restaurant for patrons to experience. The boys got up from their chairs to witness the attraction as the Tarpon splashed frantically and made a rush for the prize when the Chef threw the bucket of fish over the railing.

After sitting back down the boys reviewed the menu and ordered their drinks. After flipping through the menu, Bobby noticed a note fall from the pages. He opened the note and glanced in shock as he looked up at Luke.

"What is it?" Luke said as he looked at him with curiosity.

Bobby handed him the note that read "DANGER, DON'T BECOME FISH FOOD."

Both boys looked around the restaurant to spot anyone that might look suspicious. The first thought that ran through their minds was Gus and his companion. After not spotting either of the men in the restaurant, they turned their attention to the note.

"What do you think this means?" Bobby asked annoyed.

"Someone doesn't want us to look for that plane, "Luke replied, still looking around the restaurant.

"Excuse me." Bobby asked, getting the waiter's attention.

"Yes sir, may I help you?" The young waiter responded.

"Did you by chance happen to see anyone place a note at our table in the last five or ten minutes?" Luke inquired.

The waiter gave an expression of surprise at the request from the boys.

"No sir, is there something wrong with the menu?" He asked.

"Someone left us a warning." Bobby said annoyed, showing the waiter the note.

"Let me get the manager sir," the waiter replied, and hurried off to the back of the kitchen.

A few minutes later a man approached their table who was a tall gentleman with thinning hair and appeared to be in his early forties.

"Gentlemen, good evening, welcome to The Grand Wharf, "the man said.

"Our sincere apologies for the mishap with the menu. Please allow us to pay for your meals this evening."

"That's not necessary, but that is very kind of you." Bobby said.

The rest of the meal was uneventful, and the boys continued to scan the restaurant for any suspicious activity.

After dinner the boys left to sit out on beach chairs outside the restaurant and enjoy the peaceful sounds of the waters and the full moonlight.

"This is the life!" Luke announced, rubbing his stomach.

"I could get used to this." Bobby smiled.

They went back to their jeep and slowly made their way down W Bay Road back to their hotel. On the ride back they discussed the case.

"I'm still baffled by the note that was left for us." Luke said.

"Me too. I wonder what the real meaning behind it was?" Bobby replied.

"Someone doesn't want us here, that's for sure." Luke replied.

Upon entering the lobby, they noticed a familiar face checking in.

"Dad!" Luke shouted excitedly.

Turning his head around he embraced both of his sons with a warm hug.

"What are you doing here?" Bobby asked excitedly.

"Well, I thought I might give you a hand. I know the Caymans very well and can get some contacts here involved in the search."

"That's great!" Luke said hugging his father again.

Turning back to the front desk agent, he signed his papers.

"Thanks Frank, give my best to Hunter." Mr. Robinson shook his hand.

"Will do Ted, welcome back." Frank replied.

The boys grabbed Mr. Robinson's bags and walked him to his hotel room. After dropping his bags in his room, he went down to his sons' hotel room, and they sat on the balcony.

"Fill me in on what's going on?" He smiled. Ted Robinson was very proud of his sons. Bobby and Luke, who seemed to have his talents for sleuthing, often aided him in his cases and sometimes the cases crossed paths.

"Well tonight was a wake-up call." Luke said sarcastically.

"What do you mean?" His father inquired.

The boys brought him up to speed on the evening's activities and the note left in their menu.

With a smile on his face and settling into his chair on this warm breezy night, he looked at his sons with great interest.

"Wait, let's start from the moment you arrived." he spoke.

The boys sat and told their father everything that had happened from the moment they arrived on the island. Mr. Robinson was not surprised to hear about the incidents that took place and advised the boys moving forward that they would need to watch their every move.

After a long conversation and setting up plans for the boat excursion to the smaller islands all three said goodnight and went to bed exhausted. The next day the met in the hotel restaurant for breakfast.

"I am going to check on a few things and then will meet you at Dive Tek to meet Darren." Ted said to his boys.

"Meet us at 11:00am and we can compare notes. Do you have the address?" Bobby said.

"I'm pretty sure I know where it is." his father replied smiling.

After enjoying a hearty breakfast buffet, the group made their separate ways.

"Where are you boys headed now?" Ted asked, shaking hands with his sons.

"We are headed back to The Grand Wharf to see if we can pick up any clues that might be in the parking lot." Luke replied.

"Good idea, it was dark when you left so something might have dropped on the ground." Ted remarked.

The young detectives made their way back into George Town. Off in the distance they could see three large cruise ships. Shuttle boats began coming into port to drop off passengers for daily excursions.

"I'm glad we got our appointment with Darren when we did otherwise it would have been sold out." Bobby said as they cruised into town.

"Yeah, me too. That's a lot of people coming ashore." Luke replied.

George Town is a popular port of call and shopping district in Grand Cayman for the cruise ship industry. Activities that are available for tourists include snorkeling, scuba diving as well as shopping and dining.

Both boys looked around carefully for anything suspicious in the parking lot.

Since the restaurant was closed until dinnertime, they worked their way around the beach area. Not a single clue was uncovered as to the owner of the mysterious note.

A few minutes past eleven o'clock they met up with their father at the Dive Tek offices. It was a three story multi office building situated between a resort and condominiums with an extended boat ramp located on the northwestern part of the island. They met with Darren and filled out all the forms they would need for the dive that day.

"Darren, are we headed to the last known location of the plane and where we think it is?" Bobby asked.

"I think it's best for us to get a dive in today, but not to search for the plane. I have a better idea." He replied smiling.

"Boys, they have a former U.S. Navy submarine rescue vessel called the USS Kittiwake, "Ted Robinson explained, "that was brought here in 2011 and was sunk off Seven Mile Beach. The purpose of using the ship was to form a new artificial reef."

"You know what it is famous for?" Darren asked.

"Let me guess, a famous battle?" Luke chimed in.

"Good guess, but no, it recovered the black box from the Space Shuttle Challenger disaster." Darren replied.

"It originally was assigned to support and rescue duty with Submarine Squadron 6." Ted said, "The submarine rescue ship accompanied submarines during sea trials and maneuvers to monitor dive operations, practice underwater rescue procedures and recover practice torpedoes."

"Wow, that's a lot for this ship, can't wait to see it." Bobby said excitedly.

"There is one condition on our dive." Darren interjected.

"What's that?" Luke asked.

"No divers are allowed to touch or take anything from the dive site." he said.

"We most definitely would respect any sunken ships." Luke promised.

The boys and their father checked their gear with Darren and loaded supplies onto the Dive Tek boat. It would be a five-minute boat ride out to the wreck site which sat six hundred yards offshore. During the boat ride Darren explained to the boys and the other passengers the history of the USS Kittiwake and how the boat made it to the Cayman Islands.

The sun was shining bright, and the waters were a cool, crystal blue which made the excursion all that much better. When the boat anchored near the ship, they could see just the tip of the ship above the surface.

After final checks and preparations, the group dove overboard and made their way down to the ship. At its highest point to the surface, it was in twenty feet of water and its lowest point reached seventy feet.

The ship had panels cut out of both sides to allow for easy access to explore the ship. The boys who were experienced divers took in the majesty of the beautiful ship.

After about twenty minutes of exploring the shipwreck, Darren motioned to the group that it was getting time to head to the surface.

Bobby wanted to get a closer look and motioned to Luke with his hand indicating five minutes.

Bobby checked his air supply and knew it was getting low, so he knew he only had a few minutes. As he entered the ship, he spotted another diver going in and out of rooms but could not identify them as a member of his diving group.

In a sudden change of movement, the other diver quickly approached Bobby with a knife. A struggle ensued and the mysterious diver cut Bobby's air hose line. Panic set in and Bobby got loose and quickly kicked his way to the surface. With his lungs feeling like they were on fire he reached the surface just in time before he knew he would pass out.

Scrambling around at the surface, Luke noticed his brother in trouble and raced to the end of the boat.

"Darren, come quickly, Bobby's in trouble!" Luke shouted in alarm.

Dashing across the boat, with their father in tow, he reached the end and helped pull Bobby onboard the ship.

Quickly taking off his mask and air tank, Bobby crumbled to the floor of the boat trying to catch his breath. The startled group of passengers gathered around the troubled youth with the look of horror on their faces.

"What happened down there?" Luke asked after Bobby got some air.

"I wanted to get one more look inside the ship, "he said coughing, "and I noticed another diver also was down there. I didn't recognize him from our group, so I thought nothing of it. Suddenly, whoever it was came out of one of the rooms and came at me with a knife. We struggled and he cut my air hose. I had no choice but to try to get to the surface as fast as I could."

Darren got up and scanned the area but didn't notice any other boats on the water. He radioed ahead to the main office to let them know what happened.

He got a reply that medical personnel would be waiting for them when they got back to the dock.

After catching his breath Bobby was flooded with

questions as to who the attacker might be and what did they looked like.

"It was definitely a guy, and he was probably six feet tall, and I would imagine weighed about two hundred pounds." he said rubbing his face.

"Maybe we should put on our gear, "Luke said angrily, "and go down and see if he is still down there."

"Our first priority is to get Bobby to shore to have him checked out to make sure he is okay," his father said.

"You're right Dad," Luke confessed.

When the boat reached the dock, there were medical personnel that were standing by waiting to assist Bobby. After checking his vital signs and determining he was okay, the group met to discuss what happened. They went and sat at the end of the pier looking out at the water.

"What else can you tell us son?" His father asked.

"Nothing else really, I was just curious to explore more of the ship. I kept thinking about the plane that crashed and where we could search for it," he said. "I really want to find out where it's located. That would help us with this case."

"Bobby, are you alright?" Darren asked approaching the group.

"Yea, I'm fine. The other diver just caught me off guard," he replied.

"I wasn't expecting to be attacked, I thought maybe it was a just somebody else with our group."

"I checked with our team and there weren't any other divers supposed to be near the ship today. I'm so sorry this happened to you." Darren said.

"It's all good, I just want to know who it is and why they didn't want me on the ship. Or maybe it was a warning," Bobby said reflecting.

"Tell me more about this plane you were looking for." Darren said.

The group went to lunch and sat around discussing the case. They explained to Darren the background on Pioneer that led to the plane crashing somewhere off the island coast.

"I know someone who we should go talk to," Darren announced.

"Who's that?" Bobby replied.

"His name is Thomas Kinkaid. He was born here in the Caymans and lives in Bodden Town. If any plane crashed near here, he would be the man to talk to." Darren said.

"Do you think he would be willing to chat with us?" Luke said.

"He's a good man, I think he would help you." Darren replied.

The group headed out in the boy's jeep. They passed through George Town and wound their way up the coast. Bodden Town lies in the southern part of the island near Beach Bay. They found Thomas, who is the Director of Operations at the beautiful and elegant Turtles Nest Inn. With its Spanish-style architecture, whitewashed walls and terracotta tiles, it was a location meant for romance.

Thomas was a strapping, elegant man standing at six-foot five and dressed in white button-down shirt and khakis. He greeted the group with a genuine warm smile.

"Welcome to the Turtles Nest Inn." He shook hands warmly with everyone in the group.

"Thanks for meeting us my friend, these are the people I told you about. I wanted them to talk to an island original." Darren said with a huge smile.

"The islands are a beautiful place where many people from all around the world come for relaxation and sun." Thomas said smiling. "It is believed that Christopher Columbus, on his final voyage in 1503, named these islands 'Las Tortugas' which means turtles in Spanish due to the large number of turtles that are found on the islands," he continued.

"We have been very happy with our experience here and would gladly return to the friendliest island in the Caribbean," Bobby responded smiling.

"Can you tell us more about the geography of these three islands? And more importantly are we trying to track down a chartered jet that crashed off these islands a few years ago? "Luke chimed in.

"Yes, it was never found which makes it more of a mystery," Mr. Robinson said.

"The islands are peaks of an undersea mountain range called the Cayman Ridge, "Thomas began, "so imagine a flat surface all the way across." He drew them a picture of what it would look like. "The Cayman Ridge is on the northern margin of the of Cayman Trough. It extends from the Sierra Maestra in the east to the Misteriosa Bank in the West which is roughly about 930 miles."

"So, this plane could be lying in the trough?" Bobby asked.

"Not exactly. The famous Cayman Wall runs around the island and drops to three thousand feet in places. It boasts 4 walls: east, north, west, and south. At any time, there is always one wall to dive. The wall starts from forty-five to seventy feet in most places. The Cayman Trench or Trough is 5 miles deep. It is a thousand miles long and sixty miles wide. It is the deepest part of the Caribbean Sea maxing out at five miles deep, stretching from the southeastern end of Cuba to near Belize."

"The relatively narrow trough trends east-northeast to west-southwest and has a maximum depth of 25,000 feet, the deepest point in the Caribbean Sea. If the currents drifted the plane, it could have gone down the trough and you would never find it," he said soberly.

CHAPTER 7

DISCOVERY

The boys' expressions must have said it all. If the plane did slide off the mountain range, they would never solve the case. There would be only one way to find out for sure, and that would be an expedition out to its last known location which was about forty nautical miles off the East End of the island. It departed from Owen Roberts International Airport then lost radio contact.

"Darren, we would like to take a boat out to its last destination, "Mr. Robinson said, "how can we make this happen?"

"We can go tomorrow morning. I know our tour schedule is light," he replied.

"Boys, I think tomorrow is our only shot at this. Let's get everything in order and be ready to go at sunrise," Mr. Robinson suggested.

Thomas invited the group to enjoy an authentic Caribbean café called Cimbocca, which is in the town of Savannah which was a short drive away. The group sat around and sampled a Caribbean roti, or rolled sandwich, with succulent Jerk chicken and curried vegetables in a fire-roasted flat bread. After lunch, the group discussed the case further.

Both boys continued to scan the area around Cimbocca for any signs of eaves droppers. This boat search needed to be a mission that had no surprises and with a group of helpers that would lead them to solve the case. After everyone said goodbye, the boys and their father headed back to the hotel.

During the car ride the group agreed to do more research once they got back to the hotel on the circumstances of the plane crash to be ready for the morning excursion.

"I found the report from the air traffic control tower's last contact with Avery's plane. It goes into detail the conversation with the tower." Luke said, reading the report.

"Does it say where the plane lost contact?" Bobby asked.

"I'd like to know if it is near one of the smaller islands" Mr. Robinson jumped in.

Bobby and Ted gathered around Luke as he read the report.

The aircraft, a Piper PA-23 Apache took off from Owen Roberts International Airport. The visibility was twenty-five miles with sunny skies. The pilot was in contact with the tower after takeoff. After about fifteen minutes the pilot pulled up sharply. Just as the pilot throttled forward for more power, the engines stalled and sputtered, then quit completely.

The pilot radioed the tower and received instructions to immediately lower the nose in an effort to keep flying speed. He was instructed to switch fuel tanks and pump the throttle again, but the engines failed to react. He continued to manipulate the fuel valves, mixture control, and throttle but continued to lose altitude. The tower reported lost contact at 1:25pm.

"Wow, that is incredible!" Bobby said.

"Avery was a skilled pilot, I'm sure he did a pre-flight check." Mr. Robinson said soberly.

"So, the first question is sabotage? The second question would be why he pulled up sharply?"

"My thoughts exactly, but unless we find the plane, "Luke chimed in, "we will never know the answers."

"How long does the black box function underwater?" Bobby asked.

"Thirty days." His father replied as he walked back and forth.

"Okay, so we know he was only ten minutes out, but which direction did he take off from? Which runway? "Luke asked.

"There is only one runway in and out of Grand Cayman," Mr. Robinson said smiling.

"You are right Dad; I should have known that." Luke said, turning red.

Luke continued to do research on the aircraft. Bobby and Mr. Robinson worked on the logistics angle figuring the plane's airspeed and distance to Little Cayman.

"There has to be a record of contact from the airport on Little Cayman." Bobby said.

Edward Bodden Airfield, also known as Little Cayman Airport, is a thirty-five-minute airplane ride from Owen Roberts International Airport. Bobby and his father tallied the distance the plane would have travelled and would have put it just off the Grand Cayman coast around the towns of Gun Bay or Barefoot Beach.

"At an airspeed of 85 mph and an altitude of around 2,000 feet, that would have put them somewhere around here," Bobby said, showing the others a map of Grand Cayman.

"I have a question?" Luke proposed.

"What's that?" His father responded.

"Does the Cayman Islands have a Coast Guard like we do in the states?"

Mr. Robinson pulled out a file from his laptop bag and read his findings on the Cayman Islands. "According to my notes it says, 'The defense of the Cayman Islands is the responsibility of the United Kingdom which regularly sends Royal Navy or Royal Fleet Auxiliary ships," Ted said, "as a part of Atlantic Patrol (NORTH) tasking. These ships' main mission in the region is to maintain British Sovereignty for the Overseas Territories, humanitarian aid and disaster relief during disasters such as hurricanes, which are common in the area, and for counter-narcotic operations. In 2018 the Peoples Progressive Movement (PPM) led Coalition government pledged to form a Coast Guard to protect the interests of the Islands, especially in terms of illegal immigration and illegal drug importation as well as Search and Rescue. In October 2021 the Cayman Islands Parliament passed the Cayman Islands Coast Guard Act thus establishing the Cayman Islands Coast Guard as a uniformed and disciplined department of the government.'

"So, they didn't have any search and rescue at the time of the accident?" Bobby replied.

"The British Government would have had to send the Royal Navy to investigate," he said.

"I wonder if any investigation was done. They would have to, right?" Bobby said perplexed.

"Let me get my other notes. I do remember an investigation." Mr. Robinson replied.

"Here is an article from 2018. It says, *'Accident investigators arrived from London in Grand Cayman on Thursday morning to begin their investigation and search into the fatal crash last Sunday.*

The three investigators are from the UK's Air Accident

Investigative Branch, the agency that is responsible for looking into aircraft incidents in British Territory.

Mr. Edwin Hedgepeth was quoted as saying he was unsure of the last time an air accident investigation had taken place in the Cayman Islands.

The Royal Cayman Islands Police Service did a search of the immediate area over Barefoot Beach and Gun Bay in search of the Piper aircraft but found no evidence on land. The plane's last reported contact was around 1:30pm.

As of press time it is still unclear whether the twin-engine aircraft was having mechanical problems shortly after take-off and forcing it to return to Owen Roberts International airport or try to land on Little Cayman.'

"Well, without the plane or the black box we will never know," Bobby said dejected.

"The article makes no mention of finding the plane," Luke interjected.

"And with the years having gone by there would not be any evidence of the plane on land near either of those beaches." Mr. Robinson added.

The group sat and discussed the next day's dive. Since it would be just the four of them searching for the plane without any underwater radar equipment, the task was going to be much harder than they originally thought.

"What happens if we get lucky and do find the plane?" Bobby asked.

"Then we would report our findings to the authorities," Mr. Robinson replied. "Then it would open the investigation up again and the Coast Guard and Royal Navy take over."

The group did last minute checks before going to bed. The next day, they met Darren at the Dive Tek office at 6am. The boat was loaded up with their scuba diving gear and they headed out around West Bay and then east towards Barefoot

Beach. The morning sun was rising, and the warm orange glow danced off the waves.

The boat driver took them up along the coastline along Rum Point making their way past Old Man Bay. They discovered in their search houses lay scattered along the coast.

Once they reached Barefoot Beach which was a public beach, they decided to anchor the boat and go along the beach searching for clues.

Darren lowered the smaller boat into the water. Bobby and Luke proceeded to row up to the shoreline. Bobby brought the boat onto the sand and tied it to a strong branch.

"Now what do we do?" His brother asked, looking around.

"Let's go up and down the beach and see if we come across anything." Bobby replied.

"It's a fantastic view, "he called as they went in separate directions. "I can see all the way up the bay."

"Any sign of the plane?" Mr. Robinson called out.

The reply was negative to his question, but Bobby and Luke continued to gaze around in every direction. Suddenly Luke cried out:

"I see something in the trees about twenty yards from the shore," he said, pointing in the direction of the path leading to the road. "Maybe it's a part of the plane."

Both boys ran in that direction and walked carefully through the brush.

Deep within the trees Luke pulled down what looked to be a part of a plane.

"You know what this is?" Bobby said excitedly.

"I do, it looks like a stabilizer from a small aircraft," he replied.

"So, this means it did crash here? But there is no other evidence, or at least other evidence we can see," Bobby said.

"Well, we can't be for certain it's the Piper," Luke offered.

Soon the boys were joined by Mr. Robinson and Darren on the shore. The group continued to walk around. After thoroughly searching the area, they concluded this was the only clue to start with.

"Boys, this is a tremendous find," Mr. Robinson said patting his boys on the shoulder.

"Is it the clue you were looking for?" Darren asked excitedly.

"We aren't sure yet, but something is not right about this clue," Bobby replied.

"The silver and red markings are a start. The Piper they flew had those exact types of colors. This is big clue boys," Mr. Robinson said looking it over.

Suddenly, Bobby noticed someone spying on them from the corner of his eye.

"Luke, look over by the bike path." Bobby grabbed Luke by the shoulder.

"Someone's spying on us," Luke said.

"How would someone know what we are doing here?" Darren said surprised.

The figure was sitting on a ten-speed bike looking at the group suspiciously from near a clump of trees. As soon as he saw the group staring in his direction, he turned the bike around and headed out to the road.

"Come on, Luke!" he whispered to his brother, starting to run.

The man raced off. Having the advantage of a head start, he reached the road at a fast pace.

"Hold up boys, you won't be able to catch him," Mr. Robinson stopped them.

The group took the plane part and made their way back out to their boat that was anchored off the coast. They placed it in a bag for safe keeping after looking over it again more carefully and discovering the color markings.

"I say we look around this area to search for more clues," Bobby suggested.

"I'm in," Luke chorused.

"I agree this is too good of a clue to give up, "Mr. Robinson pointed out.

"But just remember boys, if we do find more clues, we turn it over to the authorities."

"Agreed." They all said in unison.

The group donned their scuba gear and sat on the side of the boat. After checking the air tank gauges and synchronizing their watches, the group dove into the crystal blue waters.

"How far down are we going, Darren?" Bobby asked.

"This area goes down about twenty feet," Darren replied. "It's a large area so I wouldn't get your hopes up of striking gold, so to speak, on this first dive," he smiled. "The farther you go out the deeper it drops off."

"I'll be excited if we find other treasures as well." Luke said smiling.

"Just to be able to find a big clue will make me happy," Bobby shot back with a laugh.

"While swimming around we will come across an old shipwreck," Darren said.

"How famous?" Bobby asked excitedly.

"It's the wreck of the Geneva Kathleen which sunk off these waters in a hurricane back in 1929. She got pushed hard on the shallow barrier reef which is where we will be searching at. She's a cool site to see."

"Just remember the currents can get a bit strong so don't venture too far away.

Well, here goes!" said Darren as the group plunged into the clear waters and worked their way down.

The group of four spread out and enjoyed the beautiful underwater scene. Bobby and Luke marveled at the fish swimming by and all the coral. They came upon the wreck and Darren pointed to all the artifacts that lay scattered on the ocean floor.

Luke was searching all around the sunken ship's remains and trying to stay with the current that Darren had warned him about. After a while he felt the currents drifting further away from shore. He tried to grab onto a sunken wheel but lost his grip. Panic began to set in, and his group was moving a distance away.

He tried to swim towards the surface and back to the boat. He looked at his air gauge and he was coming dangerously close to empty. Bobby will have to have known he was drifting away, he thought.

Suddenly, he noticed near one of the bollards what looked like another piece of the plane. With time running out on air, he struggled through the current to grab another hold of the bollard. Gaining a grip with his left hand, he swept his right hand down in the sand and pulled up a bag with a handle on it. Turning it over he gasped!

It read Pioneer Corp!

With the bag in his hand, Luke began to swim with the currents to the surface. Upon reaching the top, he waved to Bobby and the rest of the group. They had already gotten into the boat and had been searching the area for him. He climbed aboard the boat and handed the bag to Mr. Robinson.

"Where did you find this son?" Mr. Robinson said enthusiastically.

"Well, as I was admiring all the sunken parts of the ship I spied something attached to a bollard. It was partially buried in the sand. I knew I didn't have a lot of time, so I began to dig feverishly to uncover what it was. It didn't look like any part of the sunken ship. When I turned it over, I was completely surprised," Luke said, catching his breath.

"This now proves the plane did crash somewhere off this coast." Darren added.

"It certainly does, and now the authorities take over," Mr. Robinson said soberly.

The group unloaded all their gear on the boat and made their way to the shoreline. As they drew closer, they noticed the same man they had seen on the bike before standing down by the water. He was an older gentleman around sixty with a deep tanned figure. He had a face aged by years in the sun with a full white beard.

"Good morning, "the stranger said as they approached. "My name is Mr. Thomas. I live in a house just up the shore. I assume you are looking for that plane."

"That's right, "Bobby replied as the group all shook hands. "What can we do for you?"

"I can help." He replied.

"How can you help us?" Luke chimed in.

"I remember that day vividly. It was about four years ago. Made an awful noise, enough to get me to come outside and see what was making all that racket. As you can see, there are not a lot of houses on this part of the island. At the time, maybe about five or six houses were here."

"Why didn't you say something to us when you saw us before?" Bobby asked suspiciously.

"You aren't the only group that has been in this area over the last year," he replied.

The group looked at each other and knew that this was more than just a tragic plane crash.

They invited Mr. Thomas to join them on the beach to gain more information about what had really happened to the plane.

"How many people have been looking?" Darren asked intrigued.

"You are now the fourth group to look in this area, but the first to actually find anything from the wreck," Mr. Thomas said. "You see, we do get hurricanes that pass over these islands."

"While we put away our gear and get into some dry clothes, suppose you tell us more about that day, "said Bobby.

The group put away the scuba diving equipment, then pulled on shirts, shorts, and sneakers.

They listened intently as Mr. Thomas explained what he witnessed that day. He was always fascinated by shipwrecks and wanted to snorkel around the Geneva Kathleen. He was preparing to come down to the beach that day when he heard a plane overhead that sounded like it was in serious trouble. He ran down to the beach just in time to see the plane descending at a rapid pace. It was too far out in the ocean for him to see what really happened after it crashed.

"You say you saw it descend rapidly?" Mr. Thompson inquired.

"Yes, it looked like something had blown apart," Mr. Thomas recalled. "I called the police to let them know what happened. It would take the Royal Navy about four to five days to reach the island. By the time they arrived the search area was too large, and it was never found."

"And you say with Hurricanes crossing over these islands, "Bobby jumped in, "that the current could have driven the plane further out to sea?"

"Yes, and that's what worries me. We sit atop Cayman Ridge. As the years go by, it could drift over the edge and be lost forever."

"I found a piece of the plane that was in the brush area.

I am surprised that no one had ever looked there," Luke said baffled.

"I agree, most people would only be looking in the water. But you know what you have there in your hand?" Mr. Thomas offered.

"What is that?" Bobby inquired.

"That's the horizontal stabilizer," Mr. Thomas replied.

The group was shocked to hear this and now it all made sense to them.

"I used to fly small aircraft like this one that crashed. One time, after takeoff, the rear door opened by accident. Well, I couldn't get back to it to close it. When this happens, the tail shakes violently. Most inexperienced pilots will, out of fear, put the flaps down which makes it worse. You basically panic and lose your way. This is what must have happened, and the pilot couldn't get back to the airport in time and it crashed into the ocean after it broke off," Mr. Thomas said finally.

"How long would the flight have taken to Little Cayman?" Bobby asked.

"About thirty-five to forty minutes, not long," Mr. Thomas replied.

"We must get the Cayman Coast Guard involved and search these waters, Dad." Bobby surmised.

"Yeah, now that we have two pieces of crucial evidence to back it up," Luke interjected.

"I agree boys. Let's get the authorities involved," Mr. Thompson said.

"What about those other groups that have been searching as well?" Mr. Thomas offered.

"He's right, they may be after this plane for other reasons, "Luke said chillingly.

The group looked around to make sure they were not being watched. After gathering their gear, they headed back to

Dive Tek. Darren guided the boat down the coast and headed back to West Bay.

They were cruising along at about 30 knots. The sun was rising, and the blue sky above made for a beautiful morning.

"Hey, we have someone coming at us," Darren announced over the sound of the engine.

"Is it the Coast Guard?" Luke asked.

Mr. Robinson got out his binoculars to make out who was driving the boat. It looked official from his vantage point.

CHAPTER 8

LOST PLANE

Darren slowed down the boat as the other boat came within sight of them. As the double engine boat came along side of them, he could see the Coast Guard insignia on the door.

"Are you boys alright?" An unfamiliar man shouted.

"Yes, we are, we were just doing some scuba diving" Darren responded.

"We got a call about a boat in distress," he said.

"Not on our boat, Commander," Darren said. He was becoming suspicious and shot a glance towards Mr. Robinson.

"We will be coming aboard to do an inspection of your boat." another replied.

"It's okay fellas, I work for Dive Tek, and this is our boat. We have an office just off West Bay."

"Prepare for us to come aboard." the man announced.

Three officers from the boat came aboard the ship. They did a search of the ship but did not find anything mechanically wrong.

"What's this?" The officer pointed to the stabilizer.

"This is a piece of plane that we discovered just off Gun Bay. We were heading back to the docks to contact you guys," Darren lied.

"We will need to hold this as evidence." the man told the group.

"We would like to call it in just to be sure," Mr. Robinson said.

"You can stop at the Coast Guard station tomorrow and speak with Commander Klein."

The officers headed back over to their ship and untied the mooring from the Dive Tek boat. They gunned the engine and headed out from the shoreline.

The group protested to the Commander, but his officers held them at bay as they launched the ship.

Dejected, the group decided to race back to the Dive Tek offices to report what had happened.

"Can't we radio them from here to let them know?" Bobby interjected.

"I was suspicious of them the whole time. I will radio them now," he replied.

"Dive Tek WT 1959 calling Coast Guard Station." Darren announced.

He repeated it again.

"Coast Guard Station to Dive Tek WT 1959 go ahead." Came the voice on the other end.

"Dive Tek WT 1959 confirming CICG patrol at coordinates latitude 19 degrees 2117 North, longitude 81 degrees 7 43 west." Darren replied.

"Standby Dive Tek." Came the reply.

"Coast Guard Station to Dive Tek WT 1959. No patrols at these coordinates." the voice said.

"Thank you. Dive Tek WT 1959 over." Darren said.

"This was all a trick, and those men aren't the Coast Guard?" Luke said angrily.

"Let's head to the Coast Guard station and report what happened." Darren said firmly.

All this time Bobby and Luke had been scanning the large expanse of water for any other boats that might be in the area, but there was no sign of anyone else.

"Do you suppose those men were paid to act like the Coast Guard?" Bobby asked.

"My guess is they were." Mr. Robinson replied, putting his hand on his son's shoulder.

"A lot of strange things have been happening since we got here." Luke said dejectedly.

"Let's get to the station and have that boat stopped." Darren said eagerly.

Luke found some binoculars in the storage department and trained them up and down the coast as Darren guided the boat along the coast.

He lost sight of where the fake Coast Guard boat had gone to which was by now a good distance away.

"Something about that boat didn't look right, "Bobby said. "I mean it looked real and all."

"I remember seeing another boat and the colors and insignia looked right." Mr. Robinson replied.

Darren steered the boat to the left just past Rum Point Beach and raced to the Coast Guard station near the North Sound Estates.

As he pulled up to the dock, two Coast Guard officers came out to meet them.

"Officer, we would like to report a false search and seizure." Darren commented.

"What exactly happened and where did it take place?" The officer replied.

"Just off Barefoot Beach on the North Side." said Darren as the group disembarked.

The officer led them into the Coast Guard station to file a report. At the desk was Chief Warrant Officer Watson. Bobby told the officer of the group's adventure off Barefoot Bay and what they were searching for.

"Bobby and Luke, are you sure there is a connection between the plane and the fake Coast Guard ship." He asked.

"We are sure Officer. We have found two pieces of critical evidence that we would like to have the Coast Guard and the Royal Navy investigate further." Bobby said.

"You are probably right and those men on the ship want what you found that they have been looking for all this time." Chief Warrant Officer Watson announced.

"I'll put in a call to the Royal Navy and tell them about the latest developments in the planes disappearance."

The group waited while he filed his report of what they found.

"That piece of the plane is crucial; is there a way you can try and track down this other ship before they get away?" Luke pleaded.

The Chief officer went to his radio and announced over the communication system for all ships in the vicinity of Barefoot Bay all the way around to Bodden Town on the East End.

"I knew those guys were phonies." Luke said, smacking his fists.

"They must have commandeered a ship and just slapped that fake insignia right on the door." Bobby said agreeing with Luke. He had noticed coming in that the Coast Guard insignia was located on the right front of the ship near the bow, not on the door as they had noticed.

"We will find whatever ship this was and have the men

arrested for impersonating a military ship. And will get that piece of the plane." he said firmly.

"I feel much better now that we know a general sense of where the plane is located and the bag from Pioneer is a huge piece of evidence." Mr. Robinson said to his boys.

"How can Dive Tek help you all more?" Darren said feeling obligated.

"Just working with the Coast Guard will be a huge help." Bobby said patting Darren on the shoulder.

The next day everyone met again with Chief Warrant Officer Watson to discuss the next steps in the search for the plane.

"Any news on that other ship?" Mr. Robinson said to the officer as the group came up to the desk.

The Chief Warrant Officer told the group he got in touch with the captain of ship they encountered. It had been stolen from a dock in George Town overnight. The ship's name is the *Andre Marie* and is based here in the Cayman Islands.

The chief warrant officer told the group he would place a call to the captain of the *Andre Marie* at once. The captain answered the phone and detailed what had happened to his ship. He had a deep, husky sailor's voice.

"Yes, the ship was docked for the night. We had just come from the port of Miami with food supplies, "the captain explained. "I had sailors keeping watch overnight."

"Were these sailors a part of your regular crew?" Bobby spoke up.

"No, we hire local crews when in port so the crew can get some sleep." He replied.

Bobby and Luke looked at each other with the same thought. Then Bobby asked the question he was sure he knew the answer.

"Captain, was one of the gentlemen heavyset and bald?" Bobby suggested.

"Yes, he was. He said he was a friend of the culinary chef." The captain replied to Bobby's questioning. "I believe he said his name was Gus."

After he was brought up to speed on the case they are working on, he said, "That would explain why it was so easy for him to get the job."

"But my question is this, "Mr. Robinson spoke up, "why any of the crew didn't notice that the ship had left port.

There was silence on the other end of the line.

"I'm, I'm afraid I must confess, "the captain said in a low tone of voice, "The crew were somehow put to sleep by some sort of gas. When they awoke, they were tied up. They could here men talking to another group of men up on the deck."

"That was us they were talking to sir." Luke responded.

"Captain, why were you not on ship at the time?" Chief Warrant Officer Watson said.

"As I said, we are based here in the Caymans. Our senior officers have homes here." he replied.

"Do you have a way to track where the ship is?" Bobby asked.

"All ships are fitted with a device called an AIS, which stands for Automatic Identification System, "Mr. Robinson said, "which electronically transmits the ships data and GPS positions, heading & speed to other ships and to shore."

"Could Gus have disabled it if he knew where it was?" Luke jumped in.

"The CICG issues a warning to all mariners to not disable their vessel's Automated Identification System (AIS) due to the potential for danger and the legal consequences that they could face." Chief Warrant Officer Watson said.

Petty Officer Thomas continued, "AIS is a vital tool in a

host of Coast Guard missions including search and rescue and port security. It's not only illegal to purposely turn it off but if a hurricane were to be bearing down on the island, we would have no way to track their location to help them."

"AIS is a maritime navigation safety communications system that automatically transmits vessel information to shore stations, other ships, and aircraft. Vessel identity, type, position, course, speed, navigational status, and safety-related information are included in the transmissions. Similarly fitted ships; monitors and tracks ships; and exchanges data with shore-based facilities are also vital." Chief Warrant Officer Watson said.

The group gathered around the officers, and they learned that according to code 33 CFR 164.46, all self-propelled vessels, at a length of 65 feet or more, engaged in commercial service and operating on the territorial seas within 12-nautical miles of shore. They must maintain AIS in effective operating condition, which includes the continual operation of AIS and its associated devices (e.g., positioning system, gyro, converters, always displays while the vessel is underway or at anchor, and, if moored, at least 15 minutes prior to getting underway. Suddenly, the radio speaker crackled to life.

"*Coast Guard Station North Sound, Coast Guard Station North Sound, this is Auxiliary Vessel 9637 on 21A, over.*"

Chief Warrant Officer Watson picked up the microphone.

"*9637 this is Station North Sound, over.*"

"*Station North Sound, 9637, Ops reporting abandoned vessel, west bound just off Bloody Bay Cove, over.*"

"*9637, Station, Roger, Stand by.*"

Everyone looked at each other with elation that the vessel was spotted abandoned.

"Let's just hope they left the stabilizer on the boat by mistake." Luke spoke up.

"Don't get your hopes up son, they must have had a boat waiting. "His father replied.

Taking note of the looks of dejection on the boys' faces, the Chief Warrant Officer Watson offered them a chance to tag along. "I guess you boys would like to join in on the ship ride over to Bloody Bay and watch all the action, huh? He said smiling.

"We sure would!" Luke said with a whooping cheer.

"Do you really mean it?" Bobby said surprised.

"Do you want me to write up a formal invitation? He replied jokingly.

"NO SIR." Bobby laughed.

He placed a call on the radio to Chief Petty Officer Hutchinson, and after making formal introductions, he led the group to the docking area. He excused himself and boarded the ship to talk with the crew. After he returned, he told Mr. Robinson and his sons of the mission.

The group followed the Officer down the dock and aboard the ship. They met with other crew members and disembarked from the pier.

The ship reached Bloody Bay in twenty minutes. As the Coast Guard ship came within sight of the *Andre Marie,* Bobby and Luke immediately saw that the Coast Guard insignia was missing from the door.

The crew of the Coast Guard ship ordered the group to stay out of sight. The captain guided the ship cautiously through the waters as it approached the ship.

The *Andre Marie* was now surrounded by two ships. He got out his binoculars and scanned the ship. There appeared to be no crew anywhere up on deck or below.

Bobby, Luke and their father crowded around the captain

as he barked orders to his crew. Two Coast Guardsmen jumped on the *Andre Marie* as the ship came up close. Two others threw ropes to tie to the ship. The crew went all over the ship and after about fifteen minutes came up on deck and reported it to the captain.

"The ship is clear captain." They shouted.

"Any sign of the stabilizer?" Mr. Robinson asked.

"No sir." The crewman reported.

Suddenly Bobby saw out of the corner of his eye movement from the far side of the ship.

"Captain!" He shouted.

A small boat with a high-powered outboard motor shot out from behind the ship and took off across the water. The captain shouted commands to the smaller boat.

"Halt! This is the Coast Guard." He shouted.

The two Coast Guardsmen rushed to the side of the boat and jumped onto the ship.

The engines fired up and shot across the water in pursuit of the smaller boat with their sirens wailing.

"We've got them in our sights." Petty Officer Thomas said to the group.

The smaller boat had more power than the officer had realized but he knew that in the end it would be no match for the much larger Coast Guard ship.

The chase had begun, and the boys were excited.

The captain shouted orders to his men and communicated with the other Coast Guard ship. Within minutes they had gained ground on the smaller boat.

Chief Warrant Officer Watson turned on the speakers and spoke into the microphone.

"This is the Coast Guard. You are ordered to shut down your engines." He commanded.

They paid no attention and continued to race the engine across the rough waters.

"Prepare to launch rockets across the bow." He ordered his men.

The captain ordered the boys and their father to stand behind his men. They could witness what was happening, but he did not want them in harm's way. The group obeyed the order to stand clear.

"Fire!" The captain ordered.

A sudden hissing sound echoed from behind them, and the air lit up with a flash as a rocket made a screaming sound through the air. With a tremendous crash it smacked the water just on the other side of the speeding boat. The fugitives continued to disobey the order and raced along the water.

"Fire again!" The captain screamed.

Another rocket shot through the air with a high pitch squeal. This time the smaller boat suddenly cut its engines and went dead in the water.

Both Coast Guard ships now surrounded the smaller boat and the fugitives put their hands in the air to surrender.

"Stand clear everybody, they may retaliate." The captain ordered. Turning to the fugitives he barked, "You are surrounded and ordered to lay face down on the deck with your hands out."

The fugitives laid face down on the deck with their hands spread out in front of them. Two of the Coast Guardsmen forced their hands behind them and placed handcuffs on them. They sat the fugitives down on the side seat as the boys came running aboard the boat.

"Search the boat, we need to find that stabilizer." The Chief barked.

"You can't hold us; we've done nothing wrong." One of the fugitives sneered.

"Guess again." The Chief snapped back. "You and your friend are looking at a whole host of charges. Stealing from these men, stealing a ship, impersonating the Coast Guard, and evading capture."

"We were allowed to take the boat." The other fugitive cried.

"Not according to the captain of the ship." He replied.

"Found it!" Bobby shouted, whooping with joy. He brought the stabilizer up from below and showed it to the Coast Guard officer."

"Didn't steal anything, huh?" He showed them stabilizer.

This announcement took the wind out of their sails. The two men admitted they had the stabilizer with them in the boat. Suddenly they recognized Bobby and Luke.

The group surrounded the fugitives and started questioning them.

"Who put you up to this? "Bobby asked sternly.

The men remained silent.

"We all know why you took this from us. "Luke snapped, pointing to the stabilizer.

"We know that plane is here somewhere."

"What plane?" The man said. It was obvious he had no idea what he had.

The two men pleaded that they were only hired to take the ship and ditch it. They told the officers they were paid a lot of money with no questions asked but would not give the name of the person who hired them.

"Why did Gus put you up to this?" Bobby demanded.

The men looked at Bobby with shock that they knew who it was who hired them.

Once again, the men remained silent.

"Take them to the Coast Guard station and charge them". Chief Watson ordered.

"If these men took the smaller boat, that means Gus was somehow on the ship and got away." Bobby said angrily.

"We searched the whole ship and didn't find any more men." The officer replied.

The group headed back to the ship and docked next to it.

"Who else was on this ship? The Chief ordered.

"We're not telling." One of the men snapped back.

"We could go lighter on the charges if you cooperate." He replied.

The men looked at each other and discussed it.

"We can't fry." One man cried.

"He put us up to it, let him take the rap." The other said.

CHAPTER 9

FOUND

The men looked at Chief Watson and wanted to know for sure they could make a deal for a lighter charge.

"I give you both my word." He spoke.

"Gus paid us a lot of money to take the smaller boat and throw you off the track."

"You mean he was on the boat?" Mr. Robinson jumped in.

Turning beat red, the man nodded his head. "He was hidden under a floor in a special hiding place." The man confessed.

"He's long gone from here for sure." Luke replied angrily.

"What do you know about this plane?" Chief Watson asked.

"Nothing, I swear, "the head man confessed. "When you mentioned it, I was just as surprised as you were. What's so special about this plane." He pleaded.

Not convinced the men were really telling the truth, Bobby said, "Then why did you have this stabilizer with you then?"

"We swear, we have no idea what that thing is." He said innocently.

"We were just hired to be decoy's, that's all." The man replied.

"Let's get back to the ship and look it over again." The Chief ordered.

The Coast Guard ships shot across the water and came upon the abandoned ship once again. They boarded the ship with the fugitives, and they pointed them to where the other men were hiding.

"They were here, in this panel." The man pointed to the floor panel.

"Everybody stand back!" The Chief warned.

Two Coast Guardsmen drew their weapons and aimed it at the floor panel.

"We have you surrounded, come out with your hands up." The Chief shouted.

There was no answer.

They slowly lifted the floor panel, with weapons aimed, and discovered it was empty.

They lowered themselves down in the floor space and looked around with a flashlight.

"Nothing here, sir." The Guardsmen replied.

"Petty Officer Thomas, take these two men to the station and book them. I will stay here with the other group to further investigate." Chief Watson demanded.

"Aye, aye sir." Officer Thomas replied.

The men were led away and taken aboard the other vessel. It sounded off and headed on back to North Sound.

"Captain, what do we do now, sir?" Bobby pleaded.

"Well, with two key pieces of evidence you boys have found, it shows the plane is somewhere off Barefoot Bay.

The Chief got on the radio to announce the last known position of the Pioneer plane.

"Coast Guard Station North Sound, Coast Guard Station North Sound, this is Auxiliary Vessel 9552 on 22D, over."

Warrant Officer Davis picked up the microphone.

"9552 this is Station North Sound, over."

"Station North Sound, 9552, Ops requesting recovery operation, north bound just off Barefoot Bay, over."

"9552, Station, Roger, Stand by."

The Chief went to the map in the bridge room. The others followed behind closely as he mapped out coordinates.

"Let's just hope this plan works. It's been several years since that plane could have fallen off the ridge and could have been lost. He flipped through papers with his officers.

"Men, let's call in these coordinates and get ships out there on the double." He barked.

Chief Davis picked up his microphone again, this time with a stern look on his face.

"Coast Guard Station North Sound, Coast Guard Station North Sound, this is Auxiliary Vessel 9552, over."

"9552 this is Station North Sound, over."

"Station North Sound, 9552, Ops requesting recovery ships at coordinates 19.32593,-81.38148 on the double, over."

"9552, Station, Roger."

The ships returned to the North Sound Station and convened in the Chief's office to discuss the next steps.

"Chief, what are the next steps?" Bobby asked.

"Well, I want to review the files from four years ago to gather more intelligence.

He went to his computer and searched for the missing aircraft.

"Here it is." He said, as the group gathered around.

On Sunday, 15 June, at around 1:30pm a report was

received by the 911 Centre from an eyewitness noticing something falling from the sky out on the horizon past Barefoot Bay. It was suggested it was a small aircraft. Emergency services were called to include the Cayman Islands Airport Authority (CIAA), Air Traffic Control (ATC), and the Royal Navy. Police interviewed the witness who confirmed the report but could not provide any more details. A search was conducted extending out 15 miles off the shoreline with the assistance of the witness, however, no debris was found. A further inquiry by the 911 Centre with the CIAA, the ATC, and the Navy did not relay any aircraft beacon emergency within the Cayman Islands region.

"Well, we know the general vicinity of where to look, it's just a big cooperation with the Royal Navy to open the investigation." Chief Watson said.

"That could take days for them to get here, can't the Coast Guard do its own search?" Luke asked.

"We are limited unfortunately in our S&R capabilities." Chief Watson replied.

"Let's get together tomorrow. I'll place some calls to other agencies."

The next day everyone met in the conference room at the Coast Guard Station. Among the attendees were the Civil Air Authority, Joint Marine Unit and the Air Operations Unit. Discussions took place surrounding the circumstances regarding the downed aircraft.

"Ladies and Gentlemen, thank you for meeting on such short notice. With regards to the Apache aircraft that went missing in June 2018, new evidence has come to light to re-open the investigation", Chief Watson remarked. "With us today are three civilians from the United States who have an open investigation of their own, and I will open the floor to them."

"Thank you Chief." Mr. Robinson said, who stood and approached the lectern. "My sons and I are investigating a missing Apache aircraft that went missing in these waters in 2018. Our investigation has led us to believe this was not an accident. We have recently recovered a vertical stabilizer and a laptop bag from the ocean floor. This confirms the aircraft is in an unknown location and we are asking for assistance from the Cayman Island Coast Guard to locate it."

"What makes our investigation harder, "Bobby added, "is the unknown last contact with the pilot as well as our intel from Chief Watson that the Island sits atop Cayman Ridge. If the plane slides off, we may never find the cause."

Chief Watson pulled up on the screen the last reported radio contact and marked it with a red dot.

"As you all know these waters are tranquil and clear, but also deceptive, unpredictable as well as unforgiving." Chief Watson warned.

"We have known suspects who are trying to sabotage this investigation for their own benefit surrounding the mysterious nature of the company called Pioneer Corporation." Mr. Robinson added.

The commander of the Joint Marine Unit raised his hand.

"Mr. Robinson, please inform this group as to the reason for the investigation." he asked.

"Certainly, thank you commander." Mr. Robinson replied. He went into full detail behind the mysterious decline of Pioneer and the reason for the CEO to be traveling to the Caymans.

Mr. Stephenson who was the head of the Civil Air Authority chimed in, "Well even if we do find the plane, the black box and flight recorder will be of no use after all this time."

"We understand that, and a very grateful to everyone here

for helping." Mr. Robinson spoke. "But if we can uncover other clues from the plane to assist our investigation it would help us. Someone else wants to find this plane badly, and we want to know why and stop them."

Mr. Robinson presented a power point presentation to the group. Everyone joined in presenting their ideas and the group meeting was a success.

After the meeting, Mr. Robinson and his sons met privately to discuss the next steps for if, and when, they do find the plane.

"The leaders of these groups were very professional, knowledgeable, and dedicated to these Islands, "Mr. Robinson said. "I feel confident we can find it."

"I agree Dad. The people here have bent over backwards."

"What happens if Gus and his henchmen find it first?" Luke asked with a worried expression.

"Well son, we have a lot of power on our side right now." He said patting his shoulder.

The next day, Darren and his colleagues from Dive Tek met the Robinsons, the Coast Guard and the Joint Marine Unit. With the last known contact coordinates plugged into their computer, they headed just offshore from Barefoot Bay.

"We have a weather front coming up from the South, "the Chief warned.

"How much time do you think we have sir?" Bobby asked.

"Looking at the radar about two hours." He replied.

The boats made their way around the North Sound and headed northeast off Barefoot Bay.

"If the timing and last known contact sync up that would put the plane at about ten miles due north." The chief called out. He picked up his microphone and called the other ships.

"Coast Guard Station North Sound, Coast Guard Station North Sound, this is Auxiliary Vessel 9552 on 22D, over."

Lieutenant Jameson picked up the microphone.

"9552 this is Station North Sound, over."

"Station North Sound, 9552, Ops recovery operation heading north bound just off Barefoot Bay at coordinates 19.369576,-81.125021, Over."

"9552, Station, Roger."

The Chief went to the map in the bridge room. The others followed behind closely as he mapped out coordinates.

The ships arrived at the coordinates and began to apply their scuba diving equipment. The group checked air supply and synchronized watches then dove overboard. They swam down together and began scoping the area.

The group spread out diving down almost fifty feet and skimmed the surface moving their hands back and forth searching for any clues. They could feel the current drifting them off course. If they went too far off Eagle Ray Pass, they knew the North Wall would plunge down twenty-five thousand feet. If the plane slipped off this wall it would be gone forever.

Off in the distance Bobby spotted something stuck in a piece of coral. He swam as quickly as he could furiously moving his flippers back and forth. Moving his hands slowly he uncovered what looked to be the wheel of a plane.

Could this be the plane?

Bobby struggled to release it from the corral. Once he was able to pry it loose, he looked at the wheel markings. They looked exactly like an Apache plane. He looked around to find Luke. He spotted him swimming through some rock openings and swam to him quickly.

Once he reached Luke, he showed him the wheel. Both gave a thumbs up and turned to head back to where Bobby discovered it.

About twenty yards further they noticed a part of a

wingspan barely visible beyond. Bobby swirled thoughts around in his head. These islands he knew were surrounded by the Cayman Trench, which is the deepest part of the Caribbean Sea.

They surmised they were getting close to the hundred-yard marker offshore and couldn't be lower than fifty feet from the surface. The vertical drop off had to be right where the plane was located and could go at any minute.

Bobby signaled to his brother to go to the top side and talk about what they found. Both boys swam to the surface and looked around. The boats were not that far away, and they waved their hands.

"Captain, my boys are signaling for us." Mr. Robinson said.

The boats began a systematic journey over to where the boys were paddling. Once they arrived, Bobby shouted to the officer on deck.

"We found it!" He shouted with joy.

They climbed aboard and showed the captain and the others the wheel they had discovered.

"It was hard to see. You had to be really searching otherwise you would miss it. It was stuck tight into a piece of coral." Luke chimed in.

"Now we know for sure the plane is here". Mr. Robinson replied.

"How far away do you think it is from here?" Captain Thomas inquired.

"It's about thirty yards from here. I saw the wingspan buried in the sand. We will need to move quickly, "Bobby urged the group, "the plane looks like it could go over the edge any minute and be lost."

The captain went out on deck and conferred with the Joint Marine Unit.

"Al, they found it. But we will need to move quickly to secure it to the boats. It's teetering on the edge." He warned.

"Gotcha, let's move men." Captain Al Morrison shouted.

Meanwhile, while the groups prepared to seal the plane to the boat, Bobby and Luke made a full report.

"Coast Guard Station North Sound, Coast Guard Station North Sound, this is Auxiliary Vessel 9552 on 22D, over."

Lieutenant Jameson picked up the microphone.

"9552 this is Station North Sound, over."

"Station North Sound, 9552, Ops recovery operation north bound just off Barefoot Bay at coordinates 19.369576,-81.125021, Over."

"9552, Station, Roger."

"Piper Apache recovery proceeding at coordinates 19.391764,-75.28764 Over.

"You found it, Captain? over."

"Affirmative, over"

The mood among everyone in the group became somber. The urgency to get the plane and attach it to the boats was the most important task, as well as any recovery of bodies.

Divers prepared secure lines and dove under to quickly reach the plane. As they approached the plane and began to tie the lines to the undercarriage of the plane, one diver noticed something that didn't look right.

A bomb was attached to the underside of the wing!

Immediately the divers evacuated the area and swam to the surface to inform the captain of what they found.

"A bomb? Where? "Captain Thomas shouted.

"It's under the left wing of the plane sir." The diver replied.

"All right, everyone, time to evacuate the area." He shouted his orders.

"What's going on?" Bobby rushed to the bridge.

"Our divers discovered a bomb, so we must take precautions." He replied sternly.

Bobby looked at Luke with astonishment. How did someone find the plane before they did?

"Everyone on board, that's an order." Captain Thomas barked.

The group all gathered around Captain Thomas on the bow of the ship and took seats.

He laid out his plans, moving forward considering the unfortunate situation.

"We have a two-fold problem facing us right now, "He began. "We must safely remove the bomb and diffuse it, while also securing the plane.

"Excuse me captain, weather front is headed our way." First Officer Wright said.

"We have a three-fold problem." Captain Thomas deadpanned. "How long do we have Officer Wright?" He replied.

"About an hour sir." He shot back. Captain Thomas went to the bridge to look at the weather radar. He came back to the group with his hand on his chin in serious thought.

He got on the microphone again.

"Coast Guard Station North Sound, Coast Guard Station North Sound, this is Auxiliary Vessel 9552 on 22D, over."

Lieutenant Jameson picked up the microphone.

"9552 this is Station North Sound, over."

"Station North Sound, 9552, Ops recovery operation north bound just off Barefoot Bay at coordinates 19.369576,-81.125021, over."

"9552, Station, Roger."

"Piper Apache recovery requesting EOD personnel, over.

"Roger, Vessel 9110 alerted and proceeding to coordinates, over."

"Affirmative, over"

"Captain, if I may, my brother and I are experienced in explosive ordinance." Bobby spoke. "And with all due respect, we don't have time."

"I can't let civilians be put in risky and dangerous situations." He spoke.

"It's too dangerous boys." Mr. Robinson interjected.

"The EOD personnel will be here within about twenty minutes. Let's prepare for their arrival and assist them in all ways possible." The captain advised.

The boys sat quietly until the ship arrived and discussed the latest incident. What sort of group were they up against to plant a bomb on a sunken plane? What's still in the plane that they want no one to know about they wondered? Obviously, whoever it was would stop at nothing to gain their objectives.

"How in the world did whoever planted that discover before we did where the plane was located?" Bobby asked perplexed.

"Maybe they thought we wouldn't see it and take us out at the same time." Luke said frightened.

"Nobody is getting us off this case, I want to search this plane." Bobby said.

After about twenty minutes, the other ship arrived, and the crews scrambled to get everything in motion.

"No time to waste, get moving." The captain barked orders.

Soon the divers were overboard and attached steel wires to their gear. Once they safely removed the bomb, they would secure the plane from going over the wall.

CHAPTER 10

REGENTS RECONNAISSANCE

The divers reached the plane and surveyed the wing where the bomb was located.

Moving very cautiously, the lead diver looked all around the bomb but noticed there was no timer attached to it. *That's strange, he wondered, why did it have no clock?*

Carefully detaching the bomb and placing it in the casing, the lead diver swam to the surface to hand it off to the officers. When he reached the surface, the men were waiting.

"Be careful men, let's place it in the tank." The captain ordered.

"The bomb has no clock sir; I think it was a decoy." The diver explained.

"Check to make sure there are no more." He replied.

"Aye, aye sir." The diver returned to the plane.

After searching all around the plane, the men discovered there were no more bombs placed in the plane. Next came the grim task of confirming bodies in the cabin of the plane. The divers swam and peered in the windows. The lead diver confirmed that there were three bodies still strapped in their seats. He pointed upward with his right hand.

They swam to the surface.

"Captain, we have confirmed there are three fatalities." The diver said somber.

The captain immediately got on the radio.

"Coast Guard Station North Sound, Coast Guard Station North Sound, this is Auxiliary Vessel 9552 on 22D, over."

Lieutenant Jameson picked up the microphone.

"9552 this is Station North Sound, over."

"Station North Sound, 9552, Ops human remains recovery operation north bound just off Barefoot Bay at coordinates 19.369576,-81.125021, Over."

"9552, Station, Roger."

"Cancel additional EOD personnel, over."

"Affirmative, over."

"Chuck, assist the divers to recover the bodies." The captain ordered.

"Aye, aye captain." The officer replied.

When the bodies were carefully removed, they were brought to the surface and placed in black body bags and cataloged.

The final dangerous task was attaching wires to the plane to ensure it did not slide further. It was situated about forty yards from the edge of the trench.

"Captain, storm headed our way, twenty miles southeast at ten knots." Officer Jones shouted to the captain.

"Men, we are under a weather advisory, "the captain shouted. "It's now or never. That plane for sure will be pulled over the edge with this storm."

Crews submerged the surface and raced to get three cable

wires down to the plane. Currents began to sway the divers back and forth preventing them from attaching the cables.

Captain Thomas continued to monitor the weather radar and noticed the grey clouds that were creeping up fast along the horizon. The wind and light rain began to pick up intensity and visibility shrank from yards to feet. Out on the stern crews were struggling to keep the lines from getting tangled which would cause the mission to be canceled. Time was becoming a factor to secure the plane and keep it from skidding into oblivion.

Divers secured the lines around all three-wheel carriages and swam back to the surface.

"All set captain!" One diver shouted.

The wind and rain began to pick up with intensity. Whitecaps began to crash onto the decks of the boats as they rocked back and forth in the choppy waters. The men worked feverishly to keep the lines from getting tangled. The ponchos the crew were wearing did little to keep them dry as the mist sprayed them with the force of a firehose.

"Engines full throttle, let's move it." The captain shouted about the wind.

The Coast Guard ship began to move across the water as the two divers submerged once again with cameras so the captain could view the plane on the monitor.

Slowly the plane inched along the sea floor and further away from the edge.

"Easy does it men; we can't have the wheel carriages snap off." He ordered.

The tension in the room was becoming unbearable. Everyone was gathered around the captain and looking intensely at the monitor.

Inch by inch, the plane moved slowly along the sea floor. Careful not to snag the lines on any underwater corral, the ship eased along the surface as the wind and rain still battered the boat deck. Suddenly, an officer shouted from the stern.

"Captain, captain, port side about fifty yards!" He shouted.

Captain Thomas got out his binoculars. He noticed a seventy-foot sailboat in distress. He ordered the alarm sound.

Sirens wailed and the crew manned the spotlight and aimed it at the boat.

"Attention, attention, this is the Coast Guard. Stay where you are." He shouted.

He got on the horn to the Coast Guard Station.

"Pan, pan, pan, pan, all stations, all stations, Coast Guard received a report of a disabled vessel *at coordinates 19.369576,-81.125021, over."*

Soon the whirling sounds of a Coast Guard helicopter were hovering over the vessel. Crews worked feverishly to get the stranded crew members aboard the helicopter. After twenty minutes the helicopter was ascending and headed to North Sound station.

The wind and rain picked up rapidly and the mission was in danger of being aborted. The crew knew that if the plane became detached from the ship it would soon be lost.

After fifteen minutes the skies began to open, and the warm sun beamed down on the crystal blue waters. The divers again descended to the submerged plane to do further inspections. They entered the aircraft looking for any further clues as to the reason for the crash. They located the black box and flight data recorder that was stored in a container in the rear of the plane.

After surfacing, they presented their findings to the captain.

"How long does a black box last?" Bobby asked.

"Generally, about 90 days." He replied somber. "Captain, we would like to go down this time with divers." Bobby implored.

"Yes, please sir, the plane may provide more clues." Luke jumped in.

"Okay, but I'm having divers go with you." He said sharply.

Excited that they would finally learn more about the downed plane, both boys put on scuba gear and flippers. Checking their air tanks, all four divers gave a thumbs up.

"Don't forget, Luke, look for anything that can point back to Pioneer." Bobby said, reinforcing their reason to be there.

"Roger that big brother." Luke said grinning.

"I hope we hit the jackpot and solve this case." His brother said excitedly.

"Here goes!" Luke said, hopping overboard.

The others followed suit and swam down to the plane.

Once on the plane, Bobby and Luke worked their way inside. The plane was a mess of wires and debris. The boys searched all around in the cabin of the plane and worked their way around to the outside. All four divers were cautious to spot any more bombs that might have been placed in secret hiding spots.

Suddenly they were under attack as a speargun arrow shot directly into the side of the plane.

Who was attacking us Bobby thought?

Looking all around, the divers huddled together inside the plane. Bobby's heart raced as he realized there was no way to get in touch with the crew topside.

They would be trapped down here, and fear struck him as he knew they only had so much air in the tanks.

Bobby looked all around the cockpit while the others continued to scan the area for the sniper.

Looking all around, he reached under his seat and pulled out a small silver case.

This case looked like it contained secret papers. His heart raced as he would have to wait until he got back up on the ship to open it.

Both boys reviewed the instrument panels for any clues as to why the plane suddenly went down.

Bobby noticed the throttles were in the upward position which would indicate the plane was still at full power. He looked all around the instrument gauges, and nothing jumped out at him. Luke then joined him in the cockpit and each boy pointed to various gauges. Suddenly, Luke noticed the flaps were in the downward position.

"Remember when we found the horizontal stabilizer"? He shouted through his air mask.

"I do, but why would that have fallen off?" Bobby shouted back.

The boys looked all around and then Bobby pointed to the back of the plane.

The rear door was open.

"The pilot must have panicked." Luke shouted.

"That would explain why the flaps are down. He must have been spooked, and the plane nosedived, and he couldn't recover."

"So, it wasn't sabotaged?" Luke replied.

"I doubt it, most likely pilot error." Bobby surmised.

"Still, would have the door being opened caused him to lose the stabilizer like that?" Luke asked.

"One way to find out." Bobby replied.

The boys continued to search all around the inside of the plane.

Luke searched the rear of the plane and came across a piece of luggage that somehow had made it this far after being underwater for so many years. They continued to scan the area for any signs of danger. They noticed the area was clear.

They searched all around the outside of the plane and then made a motion to the other divers to return to the surface.

"We found some clues." Bobby said, breathing hard and taking off his air mask.

Mr. Robinson took the silver case and the piece of luggage from his son and placed it on top of the storage container.

He surveyed the piece of luggage from all angles. It still had a small lock on it which he was able to easily pop off.

Inside the suitcase, Mr. Robinson discovered in a sealed plastic bag three airline tickets to London's Heathrow Airport.

"London!" Bobby spoke up.

"How do we get from the States to the Caymans to London?" Luke asked.

"Were they headed to Little Cayman secretly?" Bobby wondered out loud.

"What about that little silver case Dad?" Luke asked.

Mr. Robinson opened the silver case and inside were a bunch of sealed documents. He flipped through the pages and his expression said it all.

"This case is now breaking wide open boys." Mr. Robinson smiled.

"What is it Dad, tell us." Bobby replied anxiously.

"Avery wasn't murdered. These are documents that were prepared for him to sell Pioneer Corporation to a British company called West Yorkshire International. They were in the middle of negotiations because Avery knew that the company was being stolen out from under them." He replied.

"The plane ride must have just been a freak accident. It looks like they were just going to do some fun activity and the unfortunate happened."

"That's why those guys wanted to find the plane then." Luke said.

"Yep, they wanted to cover anything up about the sale." Bobby said.

"This must have been the last day here and then they were

heading over the pond to finalize the sale." Mr. Robinson replied.

"So, now what do we do?" Bobby asked his father.

"We report what we found to the Coast Guard. After that, no need to bring the plane up." His father told him.

"That other boat couldn't be a coincidence, could it? Bobby asked.

"What do you mean?" His father replied.

"A setup for Gus and his henchmen to also find the plane." Luke replied.

"I doubt it. Those people looked genuinely scared." He said soberly.

" What's our next move?" Bobby asked.

"Sounds like London after we wrap up here. It's our duty to make sure the bodies are processed and sent home to their families and a proper burial is made." Mr. Robinson replied.

"The Coast Guard will need to complete their investigation which could take a couple of days." He added.

The captain informed his crew of the latest development. The divers continued their investigation and took underwater photos of the wreck. The boys filled out a report with the first officer with their findings and what they think was the cause of the crash.

After the plane cables were released and the divers resurfaced, the ships headed back to North Sound to process their report.

"Coast Guard Station North Sound, Coast Guard Station North Sound, this is Auxiliary Vessel 9552 on 22D, over."

Lieutenant Jameson picked up the microphone.

"9552 this is Station North Sound, over."

"Station North Sound, 9552, Ops north bound just off Barefoot Bay at coordinates 19.369576,-81.125021 returning to base, Over."

"9552, Station, Roger."

"Affirmative, over."

On the way back to North Sound the boys and their father discussed the case further.

"Avery was smart to find a way out, but still, who was behind it all at Advanced Analytics?" Bobby spoke up.

"Anything else in that silver case Dad?" Luke asked.

He opened the case again and took out the plane tickets and documents. Nothing else was in the silver case.

"We need to learn more about West Yorkshire International before we make our trip across the pond." Mr. Robinson said.

"Let's get on the computer once we get back to the hotel." Luke said.

"And get something to eat, I'm starving." Bobby chimed in.

The boats arrived back at North Sound and the boys filled out their paperwork. They thanked Captain Thomas and the Coast Guard crew for all their help and headed back to their hotel.

After showering and changing into clothes for dinner, the group headed to a favorite local restaurant called Grand Ole House. They enjoyed a relaxing meal and watched the warm sunset fade over the horizon.

"What's our next move Dad?" Bobby asked.

"Well, first we get to know this West Yorkshire International and it's connection to Pioneer." He sat back and spoke.

"I feel better, albeit sadly, knowing that it was just an accident, and they weren't targeted. "Luke said somberly.

"I agree son." Mr. Robinson said.

"Still though, we have been followed here and should keep our wits about us. This isn't over yet". Mr. Robinson added.

Suddenly Bobby sat bold upright!

"What is it?" Luke jumped, caught off guard.

"For a second I thought we were being watched." Bobby said pointing to a corner of the restaurant.

"I see a bald gentleman with two others." Luke replied.

The man they were pointing out suddenly laughed out loud and looked to his right offering the boy's a perfect profile.

"That's not Gus." Luke said.

"It looks like him though, but you're right Luke." Bobby sat back and suddenly turned red with embarrassment.

"You are too jumpy." Luke said smiling punching him in the arm.

"We are all that way until this case is solved." Mr. Robinson chimed in smiling as well.

The rest of the meal was uneventful, and the patrons all enjoyed experiencing the beautiful sunset.

The group returned to their hotel rooms. Bobby and Luke opened their door and jumped back.

Their room was a total mess and ransacked.

The boys ran down to their father's room and opened the door. His room was in the same condition.

"How did they gain access to our rooms?" Bobby said angrily.

"My guess is the sliding glass doors, "Mr. Robinson said. "The electronic key they would have had to get from the front desk. The staff here know us, and they wouldn't have given a key out."

Mr. Robinson went to the balcony and noticed the door had been jimmied open.

"What about the silver case?" Bobby said alarmed.

"Way ahead of you on that one son." Mr. Robinson said patting his son on the shoulder. "I had that put in a safety deposit box at the front desk."

Bobby and Luke reminded themselves of their Father's long and storied career and that he wouldn't have let anything come to chance.

CHAPTER 11

ROOM 504

The group discussed the case further as they began packing their clothes for the flight home. They deduced that Gus and his henchmen were told to come to the Cayman Islands because they had a tip that they knew where the plane was located. Once they figured out they were wrong, and after seeing the boys tailing them, they reversed their position and followed the boys. They wanted to find the plane and what was in it before the boys did and destroy it.

"So, Avery came here to finalize everything because the Caymans are a British island, right?" Bobby asked his father.

"That's right son. He knew what was going to happen to Pioneer and he figured doing it here no one would catch on." His father replied.

The next day the boys and their father arrived back at Dulles International Airport and headed for home.

They discussed the case further and looked up West Yorkshire International and planned their next trip.

The group got together at the Robinson house the next day and sat on the patio discussing the latest developments in the case.

"Wow!" said Lee who was mesmerized by all the boys were telling them.

"You guys had one heck of a trip." Tony chimed in.

"We were shocked we found the plane but saddened to find the three victims after all these years." Luke said with a sad expression.

"Well, now we know the plane crash was an accident, "Bobby added, "but still doesn't get us to the bottom of this case."

"So where does it take you now?" Tony asked.

"Where it takes us, you mean?" Bobby responded smiling.

"You mean you want us to tag along?" Lee sat upright.

"Four people searching is better than two. Dad can't join us on this trip." Luke said winking at Bobby.

"Oh man, this is great." Tony high-fived Luke.

"We need to learn all we can about a company called West Yorkshire International and it's connection to this case." Bobby added.

"We must make sure we aren't followed this time around. Gus and his cronies I'm sure are plotting something. They must have reported back to their boss that we found the plane and what was inside." Luke said.

"I guess going back to Advanced Analytics is out of the question?" Tony asked.

"Yea, at this point they must know that we know what's going on." Bobby said.

"That's okay, we got what we needed." Luke replied.

The boys assigned each other tasks and would get together again the next day to arrange for flights and hotel rooms.

That evening at dinner, the boys discussed their plans with their parents over dinner.

"Sounds like you boys have it all mapped out. Just be careful." Mr. Robinson advised them.

A worried expression from their mother said it all.

"I don't like this, Ted. I think you should join the boys in London." She spoke.

"Mother, we will be fine, we can handle it." Bobby gave his mother a wink.

"I'll be checking up on my case dear. Plus, the boys will have Tony and Lee to keep them from getting in trouble." Mr. Robinson smiled at his wife.

The hall phone rang, and Bobby went to answer it.

"The Cayman Islands were your last opportunity to back off." The caller said.

"Who is this?" Bobby demanded.

The caller hung up.

"Who was that?" Luke asked.

"Someone who didn't like that we outsmarted them." Bobby whispered.

"Let's head back to Sky Mountain and see if there are any more clues before we head across the pond." Bobby suggested.

"What do you think we would find?" Luke asked.

"That safe we found didn't just get there all by itself. Maybe something is going on around there, like maybe a safehouse." Bobby said.

"Should we get Lee and Tony to join us?" Luke asked.

"No, the less the better. Too many voices might give us away. We need to be stealth and not repeat what happened last time." Bobby reminded him.

The boys headed out again under the cover of darkness to the spot where they discovered the safe last time. Not surprisingly when they arrived it was no longer there. They drove down a side road not far from their location last time. They turned off their headlights.

"Do you really think we will find anything?" Luke asked, turning to scan the area.

"Not if we don't look. Maybe they thought we would never come back this way which gives us a good chance to spy on whoever might be out here."

They drove on down the dirt road and off to the right Luke spotted a small light.

"Bobby, off to the right, looks like an old cabin. "Luke said.

"That must be where that man and his son live who found us last time. Are we on their property?" He replied.

"Well let's not give them a repeat performance." Luke replied.

The boys parked their car in a hidden spot making sure this time that it would not be discovered. They got out and crept slowly through the underbrush making their way up to the house. Slowly, using the light of the iPhone they made their way closer to the house. They stopped and kneeled down in the bushes scoping out the house.

"You see anything?" Luke asked.

He looked all around glancing back and forth.

"No movement, but lights are on, which means that somebody must be home." Bobby replied.

They continued to move slowly and steadily up to the house. Every few feet both boys would stop and listen for sounds. As they approached the back of the house, Bobby paused and gave the sign to stop.

"I'm going to go up to the window." he whispered.

He began to feel beads of sweat pouring down his temples as he moved to the window. He peered inside and saw the television was on but no one was around. He listened intently for any footsteps.

"Bobby, do you see anything?" Luke whispered.

"Bobby?" He said again.

Bobby began to move to the side and peered into another window which appeared to be the bedroom. He saw what he thought was a shadow walking around.

Suddenly everything went dark.

Both boys awoke and thought to themselves it must still be nighttime as they couldn't see anything.

As they cleared the cobwebs from the heads, they realized quickly they were blindfolded and their hands and feet were tied up.

"These are those same kids that were here not long ago, pop." A young voice said to another.

"Should we waste them this time?"

"No, but remember that call we got? Duke said they may return and take them to the hideout until this all blows over." A gruff, elderly sounding voice shot back.

"Well, we got to get out of here and deliver the goods." The younger voice protested.

"I say when we move, got that." The man shot back. "Now, git and find those other items."

Bobby heard the door creak open and shut with force. He reached out to see if Luke was near him and felt his brother's hand. They sat back-to-back.

What other items could there be? Who was Duke? Bobby wondered.

Bobby and Luke exchanged hand signals that they had perfected with their father when solving previous cases. One finger interlocked meant wait till the coast was clear. Two fingers interlocked meant it was time to escape. They interlocked one finger.

The boys listened intently trying to figure out what the old man was doing. It sounded like he was boxing something up. After about twenty minutes the sound of a cellphone ringing broke the silence.

"What is it?" He yelled. "Okay, I'll be right there. Bring the truck around to the side of the house."

Bobby's heart began to race. They were clearing out and then the boys could finally get loose from the ropes binding their arms behind their backs. They had to find something to cut the ropes.

The door banged open, and the younger voice came in all out of breath.

"Ready to go pop." He spoke.

"Grab those two boxes and let's get out of here quick. "He snapped.

The boys heard the door slam and then the truck wheels spinning gravel. The noise faded and then there was silence.

"Luke, you okay?" Bobby whispered.

"Yeah, but my hands are numb. Why are we whispering? Luke replied.

"True, those guys are gone. "Bobby admitted.

"Feel around for something to grab on to so we can loosen the ropes."

With all the energy they could muster, both boys rolled around on the floor searching to find a way to get their blindfolds off them. Bobby rubbed up against a table leg. With a nodding motion he managed to move the blind fold down past his eyes and nose. He looked at Luke who was still trying to find a way to get his hands free.

Bobby noticed on the floor near the table a broken part of a chair. With all his might he wriggled across the floor kicking the chair up against the counter and wedged himself against it. After a great deal of maneuvering, he backed against the chair and moved his arms back and forth against the jagged edge being careful not to slice his wrists. After about ten minutes of struggling, he finally broke free.

He quickly loosened the ropes and then untied the ropes from around his ankles. He scrambled to get up and walk around to get the numbness in his legs to subside. He freed his brother and they both moved to the door quickly.

Peering out the window they noticed no car or people in sight.

"They're gone!" Bobby said breathing a sigh of relief."

"Should we look around?" Luke asked.

"Good idea. They may have left some clues." Bobby agreed.

The one level house was in disarray with scattered clothes and dishes. It looked like someone had lived in the house for some time and was a hideout. Strewn around the room were a lot of to-go food bags and empty beer cans. The smell of the house was starting to become overwhelming since the boys did not have bandanas covering up their noses.

They searched all three bedrooms. There were scattered old clothes lying all around and worn mattresses lying on the floor.

Bobby searched through some of the shirt pockets and found nothing. Luke removed a pile of clothes in the second bedroom.

"Bobby, come here quick." He shouted with joy.

Bobby came running into the room and noticed Luke holding up a small backpack.

"Guess what I just found?" He smiled wide.

"What?" Bobby pressed him.

"Flight tickets to London." He held them up.

"London?" Bobby asked perplexed.

"This case gets more exciting by the minute." Luke said.

"How many are there?" Bobby asked.

"Looks like three, all first class." Luke said, looking over the tickets.

"Wait a minute!" He said suddenly, realizing the obvious.

"What?" Luke asked.

"Those guys are going to realize they don't have the tickets on them and are going to come back for them." Bobby said nervously.

No sooner had the words come out of his mouth, than they heard tires coming back down the road.

"Quick, let's get out of here." He warned.

"Should we leave the tickets? Luke asked.

"Yes, but take a quick photo on your phone so we can arrange to get the same flight to London and tail them."

Luke took a few photos, and then stuffed everything back in the backpack. They both made a hasty exit from the back door and ran as fast as they could. They reached the hiding spot where they hid their car and revved the engine. With tires spinning gravel they sped off down the road not looking back.

When the boys reached an area where they could get good cell service, they called their father to fill him in on what they found.

"London, huh? Mr. Robinson said enthusiastically.

"We happen to just stumble upon it while searching this old house." Bobby said.

"We should research who owns this house and see if there is some connection to the case." Mr. Robinson said.

"It definitely was a hideout alright. We found clothes, mattresses, and food scattered all around."

"And you said they came back?" Mr. Robinson said.

"Yes, they must have forgotten the backpack and the tickets." Bobby replied.

"What else was in the backpack?" Mr. Robinson said curiously.

Bobby turned to Luke to answer that question.

"Just some old receipts for food and some Red Bull's." Luke responded.

There was silence on the other end of the phone.

"Dad, you still there?" Bobby asked.

"Yes, just thinking of our next steps. I doubt those men will return once they get the backpack, "Mr. Robinson remarked. "But just in case I am wrong, I will arrange for someone to scope out the house for twenty-four hours."

The next day Mr. Robinson received a call from his colleague saying the deserted house had been watched constantly but nobody had come back.

"Just as I figured boys, "Mr. Robinson said as his sons entered his home office.

"The place is deserted, and no one returned."

"Did we find records of who owns the home?" Bobby asked.

"It was owned by Frank and Alice Wright. They both had passed away a few years back. Seems like vandals had been using the house as a place to hang out."

"So, no connection to the gang." Bobby replied disappointed.

"Doesn't appear so." Mr. Robinson replied.

"So, now we need to get our tickets to London." Bobby said.

The boys secured seats on the same flight as the gang members. They began to pack their bags. This time, Tony and Lee would tag along for support.

"Our one challenge to this is this time we have no idea who we are following so now we are at a disadvantage." Bobby said.

"Wait, I do remember seeing something on one of the receipts, "Luke said.

He flipped through his phone pictures.

"Got it. The Montclear, Room 504." He added.

Bobby and their father looked at each other with confusion.

"Not sure what that means, but that must be a meeting spot." Bobby said.

Mr. Robinson went online to check to see if rooms were available at the hotel for checking in two days from now.

"You're in luck boys, only a few rooms left. Should I make it for a week just to be on the safe side?" Mr. Robinson asked.

Bobby was looking over his shoulder.

"That place looks fancy, what's the room rate?" Luke asked.

Mr. Robinson clicked on rates for two rooms.

"Not cheap, but I will cover the airfare and hotel. Meals will be on your own boys. "Mr. Robinson smiled.

"Thanks dad, we owe you one. "Bobby replied.

"Just be safe." He replied.

"We promise." Luke chimed in.

"Oh, and make sure your passports are updated." Mr. Robinson shot back.

The boys finished packing their bags and made sure their passports were updated. The next morning, they met Tony and Lee at the airport and waited in the departure area for the flight to begin boarding.

"Thanks again for letting us tag along." Tony padded Bobby on the shoulder.

"We knew you two wouldn't miss a free trip." Luke laughed out loud.

"So, what's the story with London and this room 504?" Tony inquired.

"We found the clue on a food receipt by accident. We never expected to find this backpack. "Bobby said.

"Finding out where they were headed, and the hotel was a stroke of pure luck. "Luke added.

"I'll say, now we have a huge lead. Those guys in the house never saw you when they came back, did they?" Tony asked.

"Nope, we got out there just in time." Luke replied.

"I'm banking on one thing on this flight." Bobby said.

"What's that?" Luke asked.

"Isn't it obvious? That backpack must belong to one of the three of those men and, if I'm right, he will have it on him or her. Who knows, it could be a woman travelling with them." Bobby said.

The four boys boarded the plane when their seat assignment was called.

Having no idea who they were trailing would be the biggest mystery of all, but they hoped luck would continue to be on their side once they reached London.

They settled in their coach seat assignments and placed their bags in the overhead compartment. Lee and Tony sat on one side of the aisle and the brothers sat on the other side. With a clear view of the first class seats, they would easily recognize the backpack.

First class passengers began to board the plane and the boys kept a sharp lookout for this backpack. After a few minutes of passengers getting settled and placing items in the overhead compartment, the boys began to lose faith that the people would show up.

"Bingo." Bobby nudged Luke.

The last group of passengers came on board, and as Bobby had thought, one of them was a female. All three were of European descent and looked to be in their early to mid-twenties. The taller man, who looked to be the leader, had the backpack on him and placed it overhead.

"Yes." Luke gripped his fists.

Bobby leaned into Luke.

"I don't recognize any of them, do you?" He asked.

"Me neither, but now we know what they look like. When we get to London let's text dad with descriptions and he can check his files.

About an hour into the flight, the two men got up and headed right in the boy's direction. The boys appeared to be looking at magazines to avoid any eye contact. The men did not appear to recognize the boys. They stopped at the lavatory to wait until they were available.

"Can we trust Laila on this trip Marco?" One man said in low voice.

"No Emil, but what choice do we have? "The other man replied. "She is the key to finding those documents."

"Glad I went back for the backpack." Marco whispered.

"You fool, that can't happen again. What if someone stole those tickets, we would have a lot of explaining to do to the boss." He replied.

The boys listened intently to the conversation. Bobby took out his drink napkin and jotted down their names.

The men continued their conversation, and the boys kept their faces hidden behind magazines.

"Once we get to London and meet with the boss, we can find out the plan. Advanced Analytics is being infiltrated by a company based in London. We must get to them before everything is ruined." Marco said, sensing his voice being raised and suddenly he quieted.

"It's a big city, how will we find them?" Emil whispered.

"Our spies told us a deal was going down at the Montclear Hotel. We must intercept this meeting at all costs."

Both boys glanced at each other from behind their magazines.

"That explains the hotel." Bobby mouthed to Luke.

Luke wrote on his napkin.

What does Room 504 have to do with it?

Bobby wrote his reply.

Must be the room they are staying at and it was pre-arranged.

The men returned to their seats and the rest of the flight was quiet.

The plane landed and the boys felt refreshed after getting in some sleep. They grabbed their bags and got an Uber to the hotel.

The day was cloudy and overcast in downtown London. The hotel was situated just off the Thames River with a view of the London Eye and not far from Buckingham Palace.

The boys strolled through the lobby on their way to the front desk to check in. Luke grabbed Bobby by the arm.

"Bobby look, isn't that Mr. Peterson?" He asked.

Bobby turned in that direction.

"What's he doing here in London?" Bobby replied.

CHAPTER 12

COVENT CLUE

Bobby and Luke walked to a private area of the lobby to talk it over with Tony and Lee.

"Let's trail him and see who he meets." Bobby said.

The boys watched as Mr. Peterson was talking on his cellphone pacing back and forth. After a few minutes a couple walked up and shook hands with him. The man and woman had their backs to the group so they could not see their faces. After a few minutes they made their way to the hotel restaurant.

"Okay, now I'm really curious." Luke spoke up.

"You and me both." Bobby said. "He can't be involved with all this can he?"

"We gave him that disk, remember?" Luke replied. The boys had given him the disk when they met in his office. Thinking back, they both agree that maybe wasn't such a good idea after all.

"There has to be an explanation." Tony chimed in.

"Agreed, but until we know for sure, anything is possible, and we need to find out. "Bobby said.

"Let's check in then go have lunch. But we must keep our distance, agreed?" Bobby looked at the group.

"Agreed. "The others said in unison.

The boys checked into their rooms. The rooms were on the same floor just down the hall from each other.

When Bobby and Luke entered their room, they were surprised at how nice the room was.

"We owe Dad big time for this. "Bobby said smiling at his brother.

"Oh, big time." Luke smiled.

The room was a full-size suite complete with a living area and kitchen.

The group met again in the lobby about twenty minutes later. They made their way to the restaurant. Bobby saw the group sitting in a semi round booth in the back of the restaurant. They were in luck; Mr. Peterson had their backs to them as they strolled to their booth a few tables back.

Bobby did not recognize the couple who were sitting with him, and they did not appear to recognize him or his brother.

The boys sat down and looked over the menus.

"Bobby, what if gets up and walks this way?" Luke said.

"Tony, you guys' switch places with us. He won't recognize you guys. "Bobby said.

The boys got up and traded places.

"Keep an eye on their movements and give us some details as to what they are doing." Bobby said. "If Mr. Peterson comes this way, give us a warning."

"Got it." Tony said.

The group placed their orders and talked over the game plan for their time in London.

"So, what's with this room 504?" Lee asked.

"It must be the meeting spot, right?" Tony chimed in.

"That's our guess,'" Bobby said. "So, we should check it out after lunch. The Hotel obviously won't be able to tell us for security reasons."

The other groups discussion started to get a little heated and the boys could make out some of the conversation.

"That was not the arrangement we had." Mr. Peterson said, "the payment was to be made prior to my arrival."

"The arrangement included we would find the plane first." The man's voice said. "Those boys found it before we did Doug."

"It jeopardizes the operation." The woman spoke up.

Doug sat back in his chair and thought it over for a moment. He had to convince them that what he had was enough.

He looked at them again and reiterated, "I'm aware of that. I have the disk; isn't that enough to get what we need?" He spoke up.

"Lower your voice. "The man said sternly.

"Those kids found the documents that were going to be for the sale of the company to us, you fool." He barked.

"How was I to know the Coast Guard and the weather were going to factor into this. Didn't you have a boat in the area that could have gotten them?" Mr. Peterson pleaded.

"The storm came upon them quicker than anticipated and it threw off the whole plan." The woman replied. "And having the Coast Guard as their babysitter didn't help any."

"How do we get those documents Peterson?" The man replied.

"Do you know where those dumb kids are?" She spoke.

"Last time I heard, they were still in the Caymans." Doug said.

"Well, your intel needs work." The man said loudly. "They left there in a hurry."

The few patrons in the restaurant were near them gave them a sideways glance.

"Okay, okay, let's think this through." Mr. Peterson said.

"You think it through. I want those documents and I don't care how you get them. The man gridded his teeth and stared at Doug.

Mr. Peterson got up from the table and headed their way.

"Here he comes. "Tony warned.

Bobby and Luke put the menus in front of their faces to hide their identities.

The group listened intently as the man and the woman conversed on their next steps.

"He's an idiot. This whole thing could blow up in our face. Get Francisco to find out where those damn kids are. "The man said.

The woman got out her cellphone and dialed a number.

"You know who this is. Did you find out where those kids are? She said.

"You did what?" She looked at the other man. She put her hand to the phone. "They found two kids snooping around the house. They tied them up and left them there."

"Why didn't they call us sooner?" He whispered angrily. "I want those documents. They must have escaped by now and who knows where they may be."

"We are headed up to the room, will call you back." She hung up the call.

"Let's go, we need to come up with another plan."

After another twenty minutes, the man and woman paid their bill and left their table. The boys engaged in sports conversation to act like they were oblivious to what was going on.

Tony caught a glimpse of both as they passed the table. The man looked to be in his late forties, balding and heavyset.

The woman was attractive with blonde hair and looked to be in her early thirties.

"How do we get into this meeting?" Tony said to the group.

"There has to be some way to eaves drop on the meeting?" Lee said.

"Don't know, but let's follow them to see if they go to back to Room 504". Bobby said.

The man and the woman got in the lobby elevator and the boys rushed to the lobby door and waited to see which floor it stopped at. The elevator stopped on the fifth floor.

"It stopped on the fifth floor; they must be going to that room." Bobby said to the group.

"Should we take the stairs, just in case?" Luke said.

"Yes, let's take it the fourth floor, and we can go up from there." He replied.

The boys rode the elevator to the fourth floor. The doors opened and they noticed no one on the floor excepts the maids. They made their way to the stairwell door and slowly opened it. They listened for any sounds from above. They slowly walked up the steps and noticed no one at the door.

When they reached the door, Bobby peered through the window. He slowly opened the door and looked both ways. No one was in the hallway.

They walked down the hallway and passed Room 504. Bobby pressed his ear to the door and didn't hear any sounds. Suddenly they heard a nearby door open and they knew they were trapped. *What would they say?*

An elderly man and his wife exited their room and were stunned to see the boys standing there.

"Excuse me boys, are you looking for someone?" The elderly man asked.

Bobby pointed to go down the hallway out of earshot of

Room 504. He used the excuse he was looking for someone else's room.

"Yes, I was looking for my colleagues. He's an older gentleman and she is a blonde. Would you happen to know which room they may have gone in?"

"No, I'm afraid I haven't. We are late for dinner. Excuse us." he said.

The elderly couple got on the elevator and the doors closed.

"Well, now what?" Tony asked.

"Let's get out of here. That couple may tell the front desk." Bobby replied.

Luke noticed outside the door a room service tray full of dishes.

"I got an idea fellas." Luke spoke up. He pointed down at the room service trays.

"Where would we get a uniform and how do you know when they would ever get room service again?" Lee asked.

"We fake an order and hijack the cart." Luke said.

"That's too risky." Bobby chimed in.

The group made their way to the elevator. Suddenly, the light came on above the door and the chimes rang.

The boys ran and hid behind the maids' carts.

The heavyset man and the attractive blonde exited the elevator and headed to the room.

"Get the room ready for Big Al." The man said. "If Peterson doesn't come up with those documents, he'll need to learn how to swim. "The man threatened.

"We should warn Mr. Peterson. "Luke said with a worried expression as the group approached the elevator. "I mean, he might be in all this, but we can't let him be roughed up."

"I agree, but we can't let on that we know." Bobby said as the group quickly and quietly got on the elevator.

"We don't even know if Mr. Peterson is staying here." Tony added.

"Let's go to the front desk and ask if he is, this way we'll know. "Bobby replied.

The boys got off at the lobby level and headed for the front desk. A young, pretty woman who looked to be in her early twenties was working behind the desk.

"Excuse me, is a Mr. Douglas Peterson staying in this hotel? "Bobby asked.

The woman typed on the computer and waited for the results.

"Yes, he is, would you like me to ring his room?" She said with a smile.

"No thank you. We are meeting him here for dinner and will just wait in the lobby for him to come down." Bobby replied.

The boys went and sat in the lobby chairs to discuss their next steps.

"Well, at least we know he's staying here." Lee spoke up.

"Agreed. Now, how do we warn him?" Luke said.

"We don't know when that meeting is, so we have to act fast." Tony said.

"And we have back at home what he needs to bring." Luke said.

"Well, we need to tell him, for his own good. "Bobby said. "Let's call Dad. He can tell us what we should do.

Bobby dialed his father's cellphone.

"Boys, it sounds like Mr. Peterson needs to be spared. We can deal with him afterwards. It sounds like this Big Al is in no mood for playing games."

The elevator doors opened, and Mr. Peterson appeared. He quickly strode to the exit, periodically looking over his shoulder.

"There he goes Luke, catch him." Bobby said. "Dad, we will call you back."

He hung up the phone and the boys hurried to the front door.

They got to the front door and saw Mr. Peterson getting ready to get in an Uber.

"Mr. Peterson, wait!" Bobby shouted.

The Uber drove off and quickly merged into traffic.

"Did he see you?" Luke asked.

"I'm not sure." He replied. "Taxi!"

The boys climbed into the taxi with the hopes of catching Mr. Peterson. The cars raced through the city streets passing cars until they got up close. As they got behind the Uber Bobby asked him to honk the horn. The driver got up beside the Uber and asked him to stop.

The driver of the Uber stopped off the side of the road and the boys jumped out.

"Bobby and Luke, what are you doing here?" Mr. Peterson said surprised as he exited the car.

"We should be asking you the same thing?" Luke replied.

"Mr. Peterson, we know what's going on. But if you don't work with us, you will be in loads of trouble". Bobby said soberly.

"Boys, what do you mean?" He said, trying to act innocent.

"We overheard the conversation in the restaurant."

"Exactly, and Big Al is coming." Luke said hoping to see what reaction he was going to get from Doug."

Mr. Peterson paced back and forth. Finally, he turned to the boys with a look of regret.

"I knew it. Big Al is the biggest con man in all of Europe. I'm a goner for sure unless I bring those documents to them.

Bobby and Luke looked at each other. Both were very sad

to see a longtime friend in trouble. Part of them was also very disappointed they were betrayed.

"Why Mr. Peterson?" Luke asked softly.

"You wouldn't understand boys." He said dejected.

"Try us." Bobby said and sat down on a stone wall.

"I'll admit when you first gave me that disc in my office, I was a bit shocked and surprised. "He began. "Greg Gaines and I went to college together. We started the company and then when he got big he rubbed me out."

"So, you stole the plans?" Bobby said with a look of surprise.

"No, I was just the initiator. A group of men found out I was one of founders and threatened me and my company that I had just started. They got greedy and weren't in on the stocks that Greg had gained. "He went on. "I was mad at the time like anyone else would have been in my shoes. I wasn't thinking straight at the time. I regret it now. But that disc would have gotten me out of this, and they would have left me and my company alone.

"Mr. Peterson, "Bobby said straight forward. "We understand your position, but you must help us find these guys and put an end to this."

"But how Bobby?" He pleaded.

"Luke and I have a plan. This may all tie into something back home at Sky Mountain. "Bobby said pacing back and forth.

"If this works, we can ensure your safety. "Luke said smiling.

"Boys, I never meant any harm to anyone, especially Greg or Avery. I liked Avery; I didn't mean for him to get killed. "Mr. Peterson said. He sat down and started to sob.

"Mr. Peterson, "Bobby said consoling him, "what happened to Avery was a pure accident."

"It was?" He said looking up at him.

"The plane stabilizer had come off because a back door had popped open, and Avery was too inexperienced in how to handle it."

"I'm not sure I follow Bobby."

"An experienced pilot, "Bobby began, "would have realized what was happening and guided the plane safely. He panicked and it nosedived.

The boys felt bad for Mr. Peterson but would keep their guard up just in case this was all a rouse.

"So now what do we do? I still have the disc?" Mr. Peterson said.

"Here or back home in a safe place. "Bobby said.

"I have it here with me." he said.

"We must play along and work out a plan. "Luke said. "You must convince these people at that meeting that it's back home and you can get your hands on it. We can set a trap at Sky Mountain." Bobby said.

"I'm not very good at convincing Bobby." Mr. Peterson said. He began to perspire, and beads of sweat rolled down his cheeks.

"It has to work, and you have to be convincing." He replied.

"If he gets a hold of that disk, we've had it." Luke said.

"Did you ever find out what was on it?" Bobby asked.

"It was the initial software from back in the beginning," Mr. Peterson began to say. "Big Al is willing to pay a lot of money for it."

"We can't let them get a hold of it. "Luke warned.

"I wonder if we could get a fake disc to stall for time." Bobby said.

"Well, wouldn't he want to see what's on it?" Mr. Peterson replied.

"You can just tell him something went wrong with it" Bobby said.

Just then the boys spotted the men coming down the street.

"Quick hop in the taxi, or we are in for it." Bobby yelled.

The taxi screeched its tires and raced down Victoria Street.

"Driver, get us quickly to the London Eye." Bobby pleaded.

The driver weaved in and out of traffic. The men were still behind them and gaining fast. At the last minute, the taxi ran a red light and stopped by the London Eye.

"We can lose them through the market. Come on. "Bobby shouted.

CHAPTER 13

STRANGE LETTER

The boys reached the Southbank Centre Food Market which was a lively outdoor weekend event that featured various stalls that sold street food, produce as well different types of beers.

"Luke, you and Tony head towards the Maltby Street Market. We will head towards the Chelsea Farmers Market. "Bobby said as he tried to catch his breath. "They can't follow both of us."

"Where will we meet up?" Tony spoke up.

"I'll text you. Hurry! "Bobby said.

Luke and Tony made their way to their destination. Bobby, Lee and Mr. Peterson headed to the Farmers Market. After a while, feeling the coast was clear, Bobby headed towards a street vendor, and they went around to the back side to get out of sight.

"At this point, I can't have that meeting now. "Mr. Peterson said.

"Yea, I figured that too. We will have to come up with another plan."

"We have to somehow find out what they are planning to do without them knowing we are on to them." Lee chimed in.

"It's too risky, I can't let you boys do that." Mr. Peterson shot back.

"We are going to make sure you are safe." Bobby replied.

"I must still go through with the meeting. Maybe I can have some sort of recording device they won't be suspect about." He spoke. "I mean it's 2022, anything is possible, right?" He laughed nervously.

"At the very least, we can track your iPhone. "Lee said, trying to ease Mr. Petersons mind.

"Let me text Luke first, to make sure they are okay." Bobby said. He got out his phone and texted his brother.

After a few minutes of seeing no reply, he attempted to call his brother.

"Hello?" A strange voice answered.

"Who's this?" Bobby demanded.

"Give me Mr. Peterson and your brother lives to see another day. Otherwise start planning his funeral." The man replied with a coldness in his voice.

Bobby looked at Lee with an expression of terror.

"What is it?" Lee whispered.

Bobby covered his phone with his hand.

"They kidnapped Luke and Tony!" He whispered back. He got back on the phone.

"I want to speak to my brother." He pleaded.

"Hand over Mr. Peterson and you will be able to have all the chats in the world that you wish to have." He replied coldly. Then the phone went dead.

Bobby paced back and forth nervously. His thoughts raced on what his next move should be.

"Do you have his phone tracked on yours?" Lee asked.

He opened his settings unsure if he had it or not. He was in luck.

"Right now, they are on the A308. We must find someone who knows the city roads quickly." he said, as panic started to set in.

He flagged down a taxi and the boys and Mr. Peterson quickly got in.

"Driver, please get us onto the A308. I need to catch up with someone."

"In a hurry bloke?" The driver replied.

"We must catch a car, but right now I have no idea which one to tell you to follow?" He replied sheepishly.

The driver sped onto A-308 and gunned the engine. After about fifteen minutes the driver looked back at Bobby in the rear-view mirror.

"Where to chap?" The driver asked.

Bobby kept looking at his phone.

"Got'em, he should be right ahead of us." He showed Lee his phone.

The taxi driver raced in and out of traffic. They got behind a blue Audi and noticed Luke in the back seat. He was looking back with a look of terror in his eyes.

Squinting through the windshield, Bobby considered a plan of how they would stop the car. The Audi was much speedier than the TX4 purpose-built taxicab they were currently in.

"We cannot lose them." Bobby warned.

"Don't worry mate, traffic is heavy today." The driver said confidently.

The fleeing car was a swift one. They darted in out and of traffic trying to keep up with the speedier car.

"They must be on to us." Lee chimed in.

"Unless they don't know it's us, these cabs are all the same."

Suddenly Bobby's phone rang.

"Back off or your brothers' had it." The driver warned.

"Okay, okay, just take it easy. Where should we meet you?" Bobby said.

"Meet us in the garden across from Buckingham Palace. And if you get the police involved, we will take off." The driver replied angrily.

"We will meet you there in twenty minutes." Bobby replied.

Bobby, Mr. Peterson and Lee devised a plan on how to get Luke and Tony back. The idea thrown around would be to draw out the kidnappers in a way that would force them to be trapped in traffic and then Luke and Tony could escape into the throng of people. The crowds were swelling all around the entrance to the Palace and the Gardens.

"All of these taxicabs look like, so they won't know which one is us." Bobby said.

"What if we all rode in different cabs, we could get different angles?" Lee asked.

"We need a diversionary tactic, one that draws the Palace guards." Doug chimed in.

"What if I were to be standing by the gates?"

"That's a risky plan but it just might work. They won't try anything." Bobby said.

The group spread out in multiple taxis, each with a clear view of Buckingham Palace. Bobby checked his phone to track where Luke was. He noticed that he was in the area.

Bobby texted Lee and Doug to let them know Luke was in the area and to be on the lookout for the blue Audi. After about fifteen minutes of waiting around, Lee pulled up next to him in his cab.

"I haven't seen anything." Lee said with concern in his voice.

"Me either." Bobby shot back. "I'm going to call that number." Bobby dialed the number and the same strange voice answered.

"Where is Mr. Peterson?" The voice said angrily.

"I want to know where my brother is first." Bobby retorted.

"He's standing by the Victoria Memorial with my colleague. He is armed with a pistol in his jacket. No funny business or he gets it." He replied firmly.

"Mr. Peterson will be standing at the main gate to the Palace." Bobby replied.

Bobby feared this would happen. He can't risk anything happening to his brother. He also doesn't want to let Mr. Peterson be taken. He had to act fast to save both and get out of there quickly. He looked around and spotted Luke by the Memorial. Bobby knew somehow, he would need to cause a commotion and grab both in the roundabout. With so many taxis he could easily slip away into the crowd. The question running through his mind is where was the blue Audi? He looked all around and didn't spot it. They must have ditched the car and stolen another one.

Suddenly the blue Audi came rolling around the circle. It stopped right in front of Bobby and Mr. Peterson.

"Get in now." The man ordered.

Acting on impulse, Bobby suddenly shouted at the top of his lungs.

"There's going to be an explosion, everybody get down!" He shouted.

Suddenly there was a massive wave of panic floating through the crowds. Luke elbowed his captive hard to the ribs.

The man doubled over in pain and fell to the ground. The blue Audi and it's driver suddenly bolted out of sight.

The taxi drivers gunned their engines. Mr. Peterson jumped into the car with Tony.

With the back tires screeching, Bobby's car circled around to Luke. Bobby opened the door and Luke jumped in.

"Man, that was close. Great thinking brother." Luke said trying to catch his breath.

"The blue Audi is getting away; we must catch up to it." Bobby shouted.

The taxi driver weaved his way in and out of traffic and spotted the blue Audi heading down Constitution Hill. The Audi then made a sharp right turn into Piccadilly Road.

"Can we catch them?" Bobby asked nervously.

"Congestion is heavy mate, but I'll get you there." The driver commented.

The blue Audi began to slow down as it came upon road construction. The taxi was about three to four car lengths behind, but the boys could not get a better view of the passengers.

Bobby called Tony whose taxi took Marlborough Road up to St. James Street to try and intersect the Audi from that vantage point.

"Do you see them?" Bobby asked excitedly.

"Not yet, "Tony replied. "But we are on the lookout."

"There he is!" Mr. Peterson shouted.

The blue Audi had just passed them going east on Piccadilly Road. Their taxi made a hard right and got behind the car. They could see two men inside. Suddenly, the passenger leaned out the window and pointed a gun at their taxi. The taxi driver swerved hard to the left to avoid any shots hitting them. The sounds of gunfire made a booming sound down the narrow road.

"Back off." Tony demanded. "No need for anyone to get hurt."

The taxi driver slowed down and came to stop at the intersection.

"That was close." Mr. Peterson said, wiping his brow.

Bobby and Luke pulled up next to Tony and spoke through the open windows.

"What happened?" Bobby asked.

"We ran into a little issue." Tony said holding up his hand in a gun shooting motion.

"Bobby, we got someone behind us." Luke said looking back.

The boys looked out the rear window and noticed another car idling about a block back.

"That car has followed us since Buckingham Palace." Luke said.

"You think they had some help?" Bobby said thoughtfully.

"Well, we were both on opposite sides of the street, so it would make sense to try and nab both Mr. Peterson and I." Luke responded.

Thinking of a quick plan and where to meet up, Bobby looked up on his phone a google map of the area.

"Let's split up so if we are being trailed, they won't be able to get both of us, "Bobby said. "Meet at Scotland Yard in about twenty to twenty-five minutes."

"Roger that, be careful boys. "Tony said. Then their taxi headed back down St. James Street via a few narrow alleys.

"Let's see if we really are being followed." Bobby announced. The driver continued down Piccadilly Road and looked out in his side rear mirror.

"Don't look now, but he's right on our tail." Luke warned.

The taxi driver kept looking in his rearview and side mirrors to get an idea of who was following them.

"I've got a few tricks up my sleeve, "said the driver. "I'm going to cut through some alleys, hang on boys."

The driver expertly maneuvered in and out of the side streets to evade the trailing car.

He applied the brakes of the taxi quickly, and the trailing car came upon then suddenly then backed off so as not to hit them.

The other car *was* following them and lost their sense of distance.

"Well, that proves it." Luke said.

"Get us to Scotland Yard as quick as you can." Bobby begged.

As the driver weaved in and out of the side streets, the boys made it to Scotland Yard unscathed. There they met up with Tony and Mr. Peterson, and Lee.

"We were being followed alright." Luke announced as he got out of the car.

"Did you get a good look at the occupants?" Mr. Peterson asked.

"Only that it was two men, looked to be heavyset." Bobby replied.

The group headed into Scotland Yard and approached the main desk where Sargent Robinson was on duty.

"How can I help you gentlemen?" The officer asked smiling.

"Is Captain Hartley in?" Bobby asked politely.

"He's a busy captain, can I ask what this is about?" The officer replied.

"We are Bobby and Luke Robinson; our father is Ted Robinson." he spoke.

"Just a minute, let me see if he is in." The officer went back into the offices.

After a few minutes, a husky balding gentleman who looked to be in his late fifties approached the operations desk.

"Boys, it's great to see you, come on back." The captain said smiling.

"What brings you by the station? I didn't know you would be visiting here in London."

"We are following up on a case from back home about some missing documents." Bobby said.

The boys had explained everything about the case from when they first discovered the disk at Sky Mountain and the missing plane. After the chase they knew coming here would be the safest bet.

"Sounds like the second car that chased you was a clever planned part of the first car, "The captain explained. "Buckingham Palace was the safest place they could do the swap with all the tourists around. Bobby your plan to announce the explosion, while dangerous in its potential outcome, did save your brother and Mr. Peterson."

"Thank you, sir, we both got our quick thinking from our father." Bobby said with a smile.

"I wouldn't recommend that plan in the future though, being right at the Queen's palace." He winked. "Now, what can my men and I do to help you boys out?" The captain added.

"Well, Mr. Peterson is in grave danger if he doesn't attend that meeting and provide the disk." Bobby said gravely.

"Who's making threats against you?" the captain asked.

"His name is Al, I don't know his last name." Mr. Peterson said sadly.

"Al Constantino. He's the biggest dealer here in London. He strong arms people to sell what they discovered and finds the highest bidder. He's been doing it for years, but we couldn't nail him." The captain replied angrily.

"He needs to be stopped." Luke said punching his fists.

"Easier said than done, but I have a plan boys!" The captain smiled.

The group listened intently as the captain explained that if they could somehow get Big Al to admit what he was doing without knowing it, this plan just might work. Modern technology would work against him.

"We have to get him somehow on record that he planned everything and keep a copy." The captain said.

"We could try that plan I had of being room service attendants and have a phone hidden." Luke replied.

"Has he seen either of you?" the captain asked.

"No, he doesn't know either of us." Bobby spoke up.

"Well, it's a start." The captain said as he paced the room.

"We will need to be extra careful and if the plan doesn't work to be able to get Mr. Peterson out of that room." Bobby warned.

The group gathered a few other officers into the station's conference room to layout the plan. Mr. Peterson would make the call that he would meet with Big Al at the hotel at nine o'clock in the morning. The boys would work with the hotel management to garner room service uniforms and pose as employees.

"Go ahead and place the call." The captain said.

Nervously Mr. Peterson gathered his thoughts of what he would say and picked up his cellphone. He dialed the number.

"It's me." He said, placing the phone on speaker.

"Where the hell have you been?" The voice said angrily. "You have not scored any points with the boss."

"I had to make it look like I was being captured so those kids wouldn't catch on to what I was doing." Mr. Peterson said putting up a good acting job. "I want to meet tomorrow morning and give him the disk."

"It had better be what Big Al wants." The voice shot back.

"I'll meet you tomorrow." He hung up the phone. Pacing the room with the fear he would pass out he finally said," Was I convincing?"

The boys made their way back to the hotel and requested a meeting with the hotel manager. After explaining their situation, the manager agreed to help the boys.

"What would you like our staff to do?" said the manager. He appeared to be about six foot four with bushy brown hair and round rim glasses.

Before Bobby could answer the young, petite front desk clerk said she had a letter for Mr. Bobby Robinson. He opened the letter and read it.

> *Dear Bobby,*
>
> *The dogs are in the hunt. Stay after the bone and it will feed you well. No news is the news of the day.*
>
> *Signed, Top Dog*

The manager appeared to look over Bobby's shoulder and was confused by what was written.

"What does all that mean?" The manager said with his eyebrows raised.

Bobby looked at Luke and they both gave the sign that the Manager was someone they could trust.

"It's a code from our father, "Bobby began to say, "that we all had setup a long time ago to talk in code in case the message ever ended up in the wrong hands."

"It means that someone is out to get us, and the dogs are the men that are after us." Luke chimed in.

"We are to stay after these "bones" which is Big Al and trap him." Bobby added. "No news means they couldn't find any more on him."

"I'm still confused about this meeting," Tony said scratching his head.

"So, Doug is meeting with this guy Big Al. He is a con man who buys up company plans and sells them to higher bidders, "Luke said. "What we don't know is who this company is, and Doug is going to be the key."

"And Advanced Analytics wants to know as well," Bobby chimed in. "That's where Marco, Leila and Emil come in. We haven't seen them since we all got here."

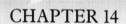

CHAPTER 14

COFFEE HOUSE SIGNAL

The next day, Bobby and Luke met with the manager and made their way to the room service office. Mr. Peterson walked back and forth in the lobby planning out what he was going to say.

"We need to somehow bug the room once we deliver the coffee." Bobby said.

"I'll be a distraction while you set it up." Luke added confidently.

"I hope this idea works." Mr. Peterson said nervously.

The group met with hotel security and would have them posted down the hall just in case something went wrong. After the boys set up the bug, they would be in a hotel room across the atrium and have a telescope aimed at the room.

Mr. Peterson made his way to the elevator and got off at the fifth floor. With nervous energy he proceeded down the hallway. He passed two housekeepers and their carts. The ladies were undercover police officers who would stake out the room while they pretended to clean rooms.

"Here goes nothing." Mr. Peterson mumbled to himself as he knocked on the door.

Francisco answered the door. He walked in and saw Big Al sitting on the plush couch near the window. Seated at the dining room table were Marco and Laila who had been on the plane to London.

"Have a seat Peterson." Big Al said coldly.

Mr. Peterson sat down in the chair directly across from Big Al. His eyes wandered to the others in the room.

"Those kids are going to make the value of your life less valuable." Al said sharply.

"I promise you I had them fooled, I didn't expect them to find the plane." He spoke.

"THEY FOUND THE DOCUMENTS YOU IDIOT." He shouted.

From down the hallway, one of the ladies spoke into her microphone.

"We need to get room service up here as quick as possible," She warned. "It's already starting to get heated in there."

"Mr. Peterson is supposed to ask them about it." Security Officer Lane responded.

Back up in the room, Mr. Peterson had asked if they could have some coffee delivered to the room and they could talk this over.

"Laila, get us something from room service." Big Al ordered.

She got up from her chair and went to look at the room service menu. She dialed room service and ordered coffee for eight. She hung up the phone and turned to Al.

"It will be here in twenty minutes." She replied.

Sitting back in his chair thinking of what to say to stall for time, Doug looked over at Al.

"Was that your men yesterday who tried to kidnap me?" Mr. Peterson stared at Al.

"What are you talking about?" Big Al snapped back.

"I was almost a goner at Buckingham Palace. Some rough shots wanted to take me for a little ride. I'm sure that I would have ended up in the Thames River." He replied.

"Damn it!" Big Al said getting up and pacing the room. "It's got to be that lowlife Grisham."

"Who's Grisham?" Mr. Peterson said with a confused look.

"Jack Grisham, that's who. He owns Yorkshire International and trying to get what is rightfully mine, that bastard." Big Al turned and slapped his hand on the dining room table.

Mr. Peterson was hearing all this but had wished the boys had been here sooner to have that bug catch all this on tape. He would have to somehow get Big Al to repeat what he was saying after the boys arrived.

Big Al picked up his cellphone and dialed a number.

"What did you find out about those Robinson boys?" He snapped.

After listening intently as to how they escaped, he exploded.

"You find them and bring them to me." He shouted.

Mr. Peterson now had a frightful thought run through his head. The boys were walking into a trap. There would be no way to warn them.

Big Al turned and walked all around Doug. His eyes were burrowing into the side of Doug's head.

"You know what I need, Doug." He said with ice in his voice.

"I can get the documents, trust me." He replied nervously.

"You don't come up with them and you are history." Big Al chirped.

The sound of a knock on the door interrupted what Big Al was about to say. Laila walked to the door and opened it. Bobby and Luke were standing in the doorway with a room service cart full of coffee and danishes.

Laila looked at the boys with a surprised expression. She knew that they were falling into a trap but couldn't say anything. She would have to work out a way to help them without blowing their cover, or hers.

"Please come in." She said with a sweetness in her voice.

The boys rolled the cart into the room and went to set it up. Doug tried to get their attention in a way that would not alarm Big Al.

"Wait a minute, we didn't order any Danishes." Laila said.

"Oh, it's compliments of the hotel." Luke said sheepishly.

"Yes, we appreciate your business." Bobby added smiling.

Big Al came around the furniture and went up to the boys.

"Why don't you have a seat and join us." Big Al said with a wry smile.

Laila turned to the boys with a look of panic. She needed to get them out of the room as quickly as possible. She had to think fast and looked at the coffee urn. In a split second, she overturned the coffee pot in a way that made it look like she tripped. She screamed out in fake pain.

"Oh my gosh, we are so sorry." Bobby said as he rushed to her side.

She whispered into his ear out of eyesight of Big Al and Francisco.

"It's a setup, he knows who you all are, get out of here." she said.

"Luke, let's get this cleaned up quickly, come on." Bobby said, running for the door.

"I will help you." Laila said as she wiped the coffee from her shirt.

The four of them made a hasty exit from the room. Before he knew it, Big Al, Marco and Francisco had a problem on their hands. He knew he couldn't fire any shots because it would attract the hotel staff.

"Get them NOW!" He shouted.

The boys, Mr. Peterson and Laila, made a rush down the hall and quickly headed for the exit stairs. They made their way down two steps at a time. They exited the back of the hotel and into the employee entrance. A few yards from the entrance was the hotel security office.

The hotel security officer rose from his desk in a panic.

"Is everything alright?" The officer queried.

Looking at the bank of monitors, Bobby scanned them to see if he could spot Marco on any of them. He saw him at the front entrance.

There he is, he must have gone the wrong way." Luke said in a high-sounding voice.

"Where is Francisco I wonder?" Mr. Peterson chimed in.

The boys and Mr. Peterson turned to Laila with lots of questions.

"How did you know we were going to be in trouble?" Bobby asked.

"I'm Avery's girlfriend." she said softly.

The boys turned to each other with a look of complete surprise.

"You mean he's really alive?". Bobby asked with his eyebrows raised.

"It's a long story, and I can explain all of it," she said. "But right now, we have to get out of here and go someplace and figure out our next steps to bring down Big Al.

Bobby turned to the security officer.

"We obviously can't stay here and will need to get our bags from our room. Can we get your assistance?" He asked.

"Absolutely. I will call our front desk and have someone collect the bags and bring them down here." He offered. He picked up the phone and asked the front desk to collect the bags from the Robinsons room and take them to the security office.

"We need to figure out another hotel to stay at that is far from here and collect our thoughts on this." Luke said. He sat down at the officer's desk and went on the internet to look for another hotel.

"Does the hotel have any good suggestions or partners that you work with to get another hotel?" Bobby asked the officer.

"We need to get word to Tony and Lee about the change of plans and where to meet." Luke said suddenly remembering his pals across the street.

"I have a buddy who works at the Royal Grand Hotel. It's a good distance from here and nobody will think to look for you there." He replied.

"Perfect, can you call him for us?" Bobby asked.

The officer dialed a number on his cell and spoke with his friend. The expression on his face was optimistic and the boys felt a wave of relief.

"He's going to hold four rooms for you." He hung up and smiled.

"Perfect, I'll tell Tony and Lee to meet us there." Bobby said. He texted the address to Tony. After about fifteen minutes a porter came through the door with the boys' bags.

"I'll text Dad to tell him where we are." Luke offered.

About an hour later the group was in the lobby of the Grand Royal Hotel. There was a romantic appeal with its warm interiors replete with polished warm paneling. The lobby had a marble fireplace and crystal chandeliers. The sweeping staircase ascends from the lobby and leather chesterfields grace the lounge and provide an intimate feel of the historic hotel.

"This is even nice than the Montclear." Luke said looking around.

As Bobby checked them all in, the group hovered around Laila anxious to know more about Avery and his whereabouts.

"All set." Bobby said as he handed out the keys. "We are all under assumed names after talking it over with Dad. The staff has been instructed not to offer any information."

The group went to their rooms and decided to meet in the bar area. After a half hour, they gathered in a back corner of the bar. It was empty for the late afternoon. They all ordered a late lunch and took their seats.

"Okay Laila," Bobby said smiling. "Fill us all in before we burst."

Laila sat back and wiped the food from her mouth.

"Avery is alive and well. He was never on that plane in the Caymans." she began to say. "There is so much to tell you about, but first I will let you all know that I've been after Big Al and this Mr. Grisham for a few years now."

Both boys' jaws dropped at what they were hearing.

"Avery is alive!" Luke broke into a wide grin. "But we found his body on the plane. We verified it ourselves."

"Well, don't be too sure about that." she teased.

"You can say that again." Bobby said.

"Tell us all about this supposedly staged crash, "Bobby encouraged Laila. "It sounds too good to be true."

"Yes, I would like to hear it as well." Mr. Robinson said as he walked to the back of the bar.

"Dad!" Luke jumped up hugging his father. Bobby shook his hand warmly and offered him a seat.

Tony and Lee gathered around as well as Laila brought everyone up to speed on the adventures of the Pioneer CEO.

She had mentioned that Pioneer was suspicious that someone was robbing the company of their data codes. Avery found out that it was Advanced Analytics and was being headed by a rival colleague and his name is Big Al. She went on to say that Big Al found out that he was being backstabbed by Jack Grisham, who is head of Yorkshire International.

"Wait, so the thief is being robbed of his own plans by someone else and it's just one giant theft ring?" Bobby asked.

"Exactly, and Avery is getting back at both of them with a mystery company and no one knows where he is or the name of the company." She smiled.

"That's genius." Luke said.

"So basically, karma's a bitch." Tony said. "Excuse the language." He said as was turning beat red.

"Yes, pretty much." She spoke.

"Wait, I'm confused." Lee said. "How is he getting back at them? Can't he just get the disk back from Mr. Peterson?"

"That's just it. Avery wants them to think he is dead. He had his fake demise all planned out when he reached the Cayman Islands. Those documents you found will prove that he was being scammed. Big Al wanted those to keep them for himself."

"Were you ever able to get into that disk we gave you?" Luke asked.

"No, our IT guys couldn't crack the codes." Mr. Peterson replied.

"And that's why they had to find that plane, "Laila answered. "The group was never able to obtain everything. They had stolen some disks and records but nothing on them would work.

"They dropped one disk and we found it." Bobby chimed in.

"What do you mean?" Laila asked, raising her eyebrows.

"It's a long story, but back home we got a strange phone call from a stranger that led us to a random safe, "Luke said recapping the adventure. "Before we could get everything out of it, some crooks beat us to it. However, they dropped one that happened to be the master disk. But none of us get into it."

"That's a huge advantage." Laila said smiling.

"Yes, but Big Al is going to stop at nothing to get what he needs. This is why he is now threatening Mr. Peterson to find those documents." Mr. Robinson offered.

"Where is Avery now?" Bobby asked suddenly.

"He's still in the Caymans at an undisclosed location. He wanted me to infiltrate Big Al's operation." Laila replied. "We need to get those documents to him."

"I would feel safer if he stayed in hiding. "Mr. Robinson offered. "But we do need to be in touch with him as this case gets solved."

"Whatever it is, has to be at Sky Mountain." Luke interjected.

"Right son. But we must first deal with Big Al and this Mr. Grisham."

"At this time, I am the only one who knows where his real location is. I will let him know our plan once we finalize that." She replied.

The group grabbed a menu and had a late lunch to discuss the next move. They asked the hotel staff to keep an eye out for Big Al or his henchmen and they readily agreed.

"Dad, how do we nail Big Al and Jack?" Bobby asked with a serious tone.

"Well firstly, we must get them to walk into the trap without them knowing it. If they don't have the goods, there is nothing we can do. I believe we give them Mr. Peterson."

With a collective wide-eyed stare, they all turned to Mr. Robinson.

"You want to do what?" Mr. Peterson said with a shocked look on this face.

"Well, obviously we aren't going to send you back up to the hotel room", Mr. Robinson reasoned. "We let them know it must be a neutral site out in the open."

"Do you have any suggestions?" Mr. Peterson said nervously.

"There is a coffee shop right around the corner. We get them to agree to meet there where nothing can happen." He replied.

"So, what is our plan of attack after that?" Luke asked.

"Well, Big Al doesn't know who I am? He certainly doesn't know who Tony and Lee are. So, we stake out the place and act like regulars."

Just then Laila got a text on her phone.

"Jack Grisham is going to get on a plane to Virginia." She said out loud.

"He must think Big Al has what he needs already." Bobby replied. "Think that's true Dad?"

Mr. Robinson had a look of concern on his face. "This meeting must entrap Big Al to admit he was stealing from Pioneer all along. I'll make a call to Scotland Yard and have men stationed outside the coffee house."

He hurried to the front desk to use the phone. He had a fear his cellphone could be tracked and wanted the gang to think otherwise.

In about twenty minutes he rejoined the group in the back of the restaurant. "I've got men on their way, now we just need to convince Big Al to meet us here."

"What if he refuses to meet us?" Mr. Peterson said in a worried tone.

"You will have to be convincing. Tell him, in a way that

entraps him, that what is on the disk is all he will need to be victorious."

"He's going to have people with him." He replied.

"We will make sure they get distracted." Mr. Robinson said, smiling.

He placed the call to Big Al. After a back-and-forth heated conversation, they agreed to meet at the coffee shop.

"All set." He said to the group. "We will meet tomorrow morning at 9:00am"

"Okay, our next move is to get to that coffee shop on board with our plan and to plant microphones." Mr. Robinson said.

The boys and their father had a long discussion with the owner of the coffee shop. They agreed to the plan. The owner was aware of who Big Al was and wanted to rid him of the area.

"What if he deciphers that this is a setup?" Luke said worriedly.

"Or he could be setting us up?" Lee said dejectedly.

"He isn't thinking clearly and wants that disc. The good thing is that nobody has been able to crack the password." Mr. Robinson said hopefully.

The group met back at the hotel in Mr. Robinsons suite to go over the plan one more time. They were joined by three members of the Scotland Yard force who their father had already checked on to make sure they were on the level.

"I think this plan will work, "he smiled. "Let's all be ready to go early in the morning. They went over assignments and synchronized watches.

The boys and the officers headed over to the coffee shop later that evening after it had closed. They made sure to be inconspicuous and went down the back alley and entered the coffee shop from the rear. They looked all around to make sure they weren't being followed. After entering the shop, they mapped out location assignments.

Two hours later the group was satisfied with the audio layouts. They performed last minute checks. They agreed to meet in the alley the next morning.

At 9:00am, with everyone in place, Mr. Peterson entered the coffee shop and saw Big Al seated at a window table.

"You have the disc?" Big Al said in a low tone.

"I do. This clears me, right?" Mr. Peterson replied.

Big Al nodded and handed him an envelope. Mr. Peterson went to reach down in his bag. Suddenly he heard the glass shatter.

He looked up and saw Big Al holding his chest. In a panic he reached out to him but Big Al waved him off.

"It's Jack!" Big Al struggled and collapsed on the floor.

CHAPTER 15

STRANGE COLOR

Visibly shaken, Mr. Peterson kneeled beside Big Al and tried to stop the bleeding by wrapping a napkin around his hand and pressing down on the wound inside his shirt. The group rushed to Big Al's side to get a better idea of the damage.

"It missed his heart, but not by much." Bobby said thankfully.

"Al, did Jack do this?" Mr. Peterson pleaded.

Struggling for breath and wincing in pain, he looked up at Doug and then scanned the faces of those around him.

"It had to be Jack. Jack Grisham." He struggled to get the words out.

Laila kneeled beside him and looked into his eyes. "Jack is on a plane to the States Al. It couldn't be him." she said softly.

With fear in his eyes, Big Al leaned his head back on the ground and closed his eyes. He was falling unconscious.

"Al, Al, stay with us. Who did this?" Doug said louder.

"We must get him to a doctor as soon as possible." Mr. Robinson ordered.

"I called 911 as soon as I saw what happened, "the coffee shop owner replied.

"It should be here in a few minutes. The fire station is not far away.

About five minutes later the sound of an ambulance could be heard softly in the background. It began to get louder and louder as it approached.

After getting initial medical treatment, Big Al was rushed away to the ambulance.

"Where are you taking him?" Mr. Robinson asked the medic.

"We will be transporting him to St. Mary's Hospital, "the medic replied. "Are you family or friend?"

"Neither. But this man must be escorted by Scotland Yard. He is a potential suspect in a criminal case." Mr. Robinson replied firmly.

"One of the officers can ride up in front." He spoke.

After Big Al was transported away, the group gathered in the coffee shop to discuss what happened.

"Do we know where the shot had come from?" Mr. Robinson asked.

"It appeared to come from the medical building across the street. "Luke said.

"Whoever it was would be long gone by now, but we must go check it out anyhow and see if any clues can be found." Mr. Robinson said to the officers.

They headed next door and went floor to floor asking patrons of the offices if they had heard any sounds that may have been a gunshot. One of the office workers on the fourth floor heard what sounded like a firecracker.

"Can you tell us where you might have heard this?" Bobby spoke up.

"At the end of the hallway, about two to three offices down." The man replied.

The group quickly headed down the hallway. There was an empty office on the corner.

The officer spoke up and told the group to stand back.

"Let us enter first to make sure the gunman isn't still in there." The officer ordered.

The first officer approached the office door with caution. He listened for any sounds from the inside. He looked back at the second officer and drew his weapon. He tried the doorknob, and it was unlocked. With tensions mounting and the group standing in the doorway of the stairwell, he proceeded to slowly turn the knob and opened the door.

Silence.

He peered around the corner and both officers slowly entered the room. They took a slow pace and walked from room to room. After giving the all-clear sign to the rest of the group, everyone entered the office.

Bobby and Luke walked to the windows that faced the street. They looked down at the coffee shop on the corner.

"He must have shot from here." Bobby noted. He examined all the windows and then noticed one window wasn't locked back.

"Don't touch it!" The first officer warned. "We will get a crew up here and do a fingerprint analysis." Bobby and Luke looked all around and didn't see any casings.

"That's strange." Bobby said.

"What is?" Luke replied.

"The gunman made sure no evidence would be found, yet forgot to lock the window when he left?" He offered.

"Well let's hope he left his fingerprints." Luke said finally.

After twenty minutes of doing their detective work, a forensics scene investigation team arrived and began their analysis. The group stepped into the hallway while this was being done and discussed the latest update.

"Tony and I combed the other floors and didn't see anyone." Lee offered.

"Hopefully the FSI can come up with a clue or a fingerprint." Luke chimed in.

"Let's go to the management office and see if anything is on the cameras. There must be something that can tell us who did the shooting" Bobby said.

The group, along with the officers, headed to the office which was located on the first floor. They entered the room and a tall, skinny gentleman with round glasses greeted them.

"May I help you?" He said with a pleasant look on this face.

The officer presented their badges and asked to see the security cameras for the building. The manager took them into the back office while the boys waited in the lobby area. Tensions grew as the minutes turned into an hour.

The officers returned to the lobby and asked the boys to accompany them into the back area.

On the monitor screen the boys could see a figure exiting the rear of the building.

"He must have known the camera would be there as he hid his face from view." Luke said.

"Let's back it up about a half an hour." The officer ordered. "I want to see who entered the building around that time."

The manager rewound the tape and the group watched people enter the building one by one.

"Do you recognize the people who are coming in the building?" the officer asked.

"Yes, so far, I do recognize most. Wait, here is one I don't" He paused the tape.

On the screen there was what appeared to be a heavy-set man, wearing a big oversize coat. He had long scraggly hair and baggy pants.

The group rushed from the office and took the side stairs down to the parking garage and out the rear exit.

Bobby burst from the back door and looked right and left. The others had followed him out the door.

"You guys go that way; we'll go this way. Look for discarded clothes." He said pointing down the alley.

Bobby and Luke began walking down the alley cautiously looking left and right into the open spaces. The figure was not in sight, but he must have dropped something Bobby thought.

Up ahead they noticed a man in golf shirt and slacks with a clipboard jotting down some notes. He looked to be in his early forties, tall and athletic.

Instantly, Bobby called out to him. "Excuse me, did you see a man come this way in the last ten minutes wearing an overcoat? He had long hair." Bobby asked.

"He went up that way." The man said pointing across the street.

The boys rushed up the alley and crossed the street. They went about twenty yards and looked all around. They found no clues as to the mysterious man. They made their way back across the street and down the alley. Suddenly Bobby noticed it was empty.

"Wonder where that man went?" he said looking around.

"That is strange." Luke responded. "Maybe he was just done and had moved on to the next assignment."

"Do you suppose he was telling us the truth?" Bobby asked.

The others had finally caught up with the boys and reported they had no luck either.

"Let's continue to check this area by the door." Bobby said.

The group continued to look all around. They moved garbage cans and assorted cardboard boxes. Bobby investigated one garbage can that looked out of place.

Bingo!

"Luke, found it." He said as he whooped for joy.

The others rushed over to see what he had uncovered.

"That man we talked to was him, I know it!" He said in frustration.

"You mean that was his disguise?" Lee chimed in.

"Exactly, he changed clothes soon after he left." Bobby replied.

"There has to be cameras down this alley." Tony added.

The group looked all up and down the alley but only saw the one camera positioned at the back door. Disappointed, the group carefully put the clothes in a clear trash bag using latex gloves they had obtained from the janitor closet.

"We will get this right down to the station for analysis." One officer reported.

"We will continue to comb the area to see if we can find anything else officer and come by the station later." Bobby replied.

"Perfect, thanks for your help boys." Another officer replied smiling.

"This case means a lot to us, and we need to get to the bottom of it." Luke said.

After the officers left Bobby and Luke and the rest of the group decided to head to the hospital to check on the condition of Big Al. They entered the lobby of St. Mary's hospital and approached the main desk.

"Excuse me, but we would like to visit with a man who

was recently sent here via ambulance, "Bobby began. "He's a heavy-set man about fifty."

"Are you friend or family?" the young, pretty nurse asked.

Bobby looked at Luke. "We, he hesitated, "are just friends." He lied.

"Well, I'm sorry. Currently only family are allowed to see patients." She replied.

Suddenly, a hysterical woman entered the lobby. She was heavy set and looked to be in her late forties."

She pushed aside the boys with a look of panic on her face.

"I'm looking for Alfred Constantino. He was just transported here. "She pleaded.

"Are you family?" The nurse repeated.

"Yes, I'm his sister. Please tell me where he is." Her voice began to pitch higher.

She looked again at her computer. After locating his file, she looked up at her.

"He's been taken to the emergency room. He has a gunshot wound." She said to the woman with a look of concern.

The woman took a step back and the boys thought she was going to faint. She turned back to the nurse with a look of shock and denial.

"That's impossible!" she demanded. "You must be mistaken."

"I'm sorry, but it is true. I will let you know more when the doctors can provide an update on his condition." The nurse said.

At that moment she made a hasty exit from the hospital and got in a waiting car. The boys attempted to stop her, but the car roared off into traffic.

At ten o'clock the next morning the boys and their father along with Doug, Tony and Lee made their way along Downing Street down to police headquarters. They made sure they weren't being followed in their taxi. They approached the main desk and asked to speak to Constable Jones.

"May I ask who wishes to see him?" the officer asked.

"Please tell him Ted Robinson, he will know the name." He said smiling.

The officer picked up the telephone and placed a call to his office. He listened for a few minutes and then hung up.

"He said to come on back." The officer replied. He hit a buzzer and the group entered the side door and proceeded through the station. They entered the office with his name on the door.

"Ted, my old friend, come on in." He gave him a warm, embracing hug.

"Brian, these are my boys Bobby and Luke. Boys, an old friend of mine."

"Great to finally meet you boys. Your father is a class act," Constable Jones said.

"We heard a lot about you sir, "Bobby said shaking hands.

"And these are their good friends, Tony and Lee," Mr. Robinson said.

"And I'm Doug Peterson. I'm afraid I'm the cause of all this mess." He said dejected.

The group all shook hands and pulled up chairs in the Constables office.

"Well let's see what we can do. What brings you back to London?" He said leaning back in his chair.

"Well, it's a long story. But my boys are on a case involving stolen company property. We think Al Constantino is mixed up in this along with a Jack Grisham." he said.

Constable Jones sat back in his chair and thought this over. He leaned forward and placed a call.

"Bring me that file on Al Constantino," he ordered.

"So, you are familiar with these two, "Ted said with a wide grin.

"We have been after these two buggers for the last four years. They both run the city with their operations, "he said fuming. "They run it where nothing can come back to them. Well, now we may just have something."

"Tell me the latest Ted," he said sitting back.

Mr. Robinson brought him up to speed with the latest on the investigation into the software theft ring that began with the attempted stealing of Pioneer Corporation data. He ended with the latest shooting of Big Al at the coffee shop.

"Yes, my men are on that. I hate to see someone shot in our city but not surprised it hasn't come any sooner," he said soberly.

"Do you know anyone in particular who might do this?" Luke asked.

"Anyone's guess son," he replied.

The phone rang and the Constable answered it. By the look on his face the group could see it was not great news. He jotted down someone's notes on his pad of paper and then hung up.

"From the look on your face I can see it's not good, "Ted said.

"Big Al succumbed to his wounds about five minutes ago, "he said.

The group was shocked to hear this news. With no leads to go on they sat wondering where to go next.

"Do you think Jack Grisham had anything to do with this?" Luke asked.

"If Jack had gotten a hold of that disc and Big Al sold it to him, I doubt this would have happened, "he began, "But if he thought he was cutting him out of the deal, he might have wanted Al silenced."

"What did you boys find out when you looked around?" he asked.

"Well, we found a bunch of clothes, including an overcoat in an alley trash can," Bobby began, "And then we saw another man in the same alley checking things over. We think he may have tricked us and stuffed the clothes in the garbage. The police took it for analysis."

"When we looked at the monitor, we couldn't get a good look at his face. He knew a camera would be there." Tony chimed in.

"So where do we go from here?" Bobby asked his father.

"Well, I think we go back to Big Al's room and look things over. He may have a clue as to what he and Jack are up to, "he surmised.

With a police escort in tow, the group headed back over to the Montclear Hotel and worked with hotel management to gain access to the room that was used by Big Al. The group did a search of the bedroom and suite area where they had been with Mr. Peterson.

Bobby and Luke searched Big Al's luggage and portfolio bag. They found hidden in a secret compartment a bunch of documents related to Advanced Analytics.

Suddenly, Luke found another compartment.

"Bobby, look!" He shouted.

Both boys found the other discs, coins, and papers they had originally discovered in the safe at Sky Mountain.

"So, we were right! The disc we gave Mr. Peterson was the last link to gaining all of Pioneer's data, "Bobby said.

"Is it like you must have all three discs to initiate the computer games like we used to do?" He responded.

"I think so. "This is all starting to make sense, "he replied.

The group wrapped up their investigation and headed back to Scotland Yard.

"Good work!" exclaimed Constable Jones. "So, the fellow was trying to sell off what he stole to Jack Grisham and his company Yorkshire. That certainly links them together."

"Right, "Bobby agreed. "But still, there is another company involved in this, but we don't know it's angle. We think they are trying to get even. Jack must have been trying to backstab Big Al."

"Wait a second. You remember that office that had that letter that was addressed to an A. Turnpike?" Luke said, snapping his fingers.

"Yes, it was, "he trailed off in thought. "Rota something"

"Rota-Vonni!" Luke blurted out.

"Yes, that's it." Bobby shouted.

"That's why Avery faked his death." Luke said.

"Wouldn't you if you wanted to get back at someone?" He asked.

"Guess you're right, "Luke replied. "But where is Avery then?"

"That's what we need to find out, "Bobby said.

"He wouldn't be here in London, would he?" Luke asked.

"Definitely not the shooter, he doesn't seem the type," Bobby shot back.

"Jack?" Luke said staring at his brother.

He had to admit it would make total sense.

"But it would be too easy and too logical, "Bobby surmised.

"Well, first things first, we have to track down Jack Grisham," Tony added.

"Laila said he was getting on a plane." Bobby said.

Bobby's phone lit up again.

Sky Mountain is the key to the puzzle.

"Okay, here's that message again! I don't know who this is, "he said.

He showed Luke his phone and then to the rest of the group.

The text was from an unknown caller ID. The boys sat around and discussed what to do next. They seemed to be at a dead end. They told Constable Jones they would be in touch and would go grab something to eat to get their brains to churn some ideas.

They all headed to the main entrance of the police station. As they passed the desk, the officer on duty stopped Bobby.

"A note was left for you," he said, handing him the note.

Don't stop off for any coffee or it may be your last cup!

"Do you remember what this person looked like, "he said to the officer.

"There he goes now, that man in the orange jogging suit, "He replied, pointing to the man leaving the station.

"Luke, there he goes, catch him. Come on guys!" He said, racing to the exit.

The man in the jogging suit dashed out the door and began to run down the street.

CHAPTER 16

GHOSTS

The unusually warm, muggy London air made the pursuit of the mysterious man in the orange jogging suit very challenging. They chased him for two blocks before realizing the pursuit would be hopeless.

"I need some water, this heat has got me worn out, "said Luke gasping for breath.

With his brother right alongside him, he had to agree.

"London doesn't usually have this kind of heat wave." Bobby said sweating.

The rest of the group caught up to the two brothers and they all proceeded to sit down in the shade.

"Bobby, look!" Luke pointed to the stranger not far up the street. He was sitting on a bench trying to catch his breath. "It's the man in the orange suit!"

"Come on everybody, let's try and catch him, "responded Bobby "Before he does get a chance to get away.

Crossing at the corner, the boys went up and finally got a

hold of the stranger. As the man whirled around; Mr. Robinson noticed it was Avery Turnpike.

"What do you want," the man demanded.

"Avery, it's you!" A stunned Mr. Robinson said.

"Avery who?" The man replied.

"Your Avery Turnpike," Bobby shot back.

"I have no idea who you are talking about, now unhand me." He demanded.

"Why did you leave a note for us at the hotel?" Luke demanded.

"I don't know what you are talking about. I have never seen you before in my life, now I must be on my way." He said, hurrying past the group and hailed a taxi.

At the change of the light the taxi made its way into traffic and turned the corner.

"I know that was him", Mr. Robinson said.

"I agree, but what can we do?" Bobby said.

Just then, Tony noticed the man staring at them from up the street.

"Hold it!" he shouted. "He got out of the taxi fellows."

The man looked both ways and started to run again up the street.

The boys ran across the street and finally caught up to the stranger.

"Why are you chasing me?" the man demanded.

Just then the man recognized Mr. Robinson. The two eyed each other and the man began to ease up.

"Avery, it is you." Mr. Robinson said.

"No, I'm his twin brother Aaron" Aaron finally admitted. "Why are you here?" he said.

"I knew who was stealing from my brother's company and I got them." He spoke angrily. "And I'm doing what needs to be done."

"Aaron, you don't know all of it. "Ted pleaded. "Please work with us."

"Why did you send that note?" Bobby chimed in.

"To get you off the trail, and to leave it to me. I want revenge!" He shouted.

"There is a lot you don't know. Let us help you." Luke pleaded.

Aaron eyed all the group suspiciously, but then wavered and gave in.

"All right, but Big Al had it coming to him. "He shot an angry look at the group.

The group decided that where they were standing was not a good place to meet. They found an empty office just down the street and ducked in the front door.

"Have a seat, we can bring you up to speed. "Bobby said.

Bobby told Aaron about how Big Al and his company Advanced Analytics had stolen most of the plans from Pioneer Corporation.

"Exactly, and because my brother is gone, he is going to pay a price." He replied.

"Not so fast, "Ted interjected. "There is reason to believe that your brother is still alive and has a ghost company."

"What do you mean?" He shot back. "Avery would have told me all about it and I would have been in on it."

"We think your brother is outsmarting those who stole from him in the first place and getting back at them. "Bobby said smiling at him.

"He is?" he said. "Just like him to be that sneaky."

"Ever heard of Jack Grisham?" Ted asked.

Shrugging his shoulders, Aaron replied, "No, I'm afraid I don't.

"He and Big Al were in cahoots and Big Al was going to sell what he had to Jack for a nice profit." Luke said. "We had thought it was Jack that shot Big Al in that coffee shop to shut him up."

"I didn't know that was Jack sitting next to him in the coffee shop. I have never seen a picture of him. I have been after Big Al for a while now. "He continued. "Things started heating up right around the time you showed up."

"That was me sitting with him, "Mr. Peterson spoke up. "I was faking like I had the disc with me to incriminate him."

"Now that Al is gone, it will be more difficult to find out his true intentions."

"I only wanted to scare him; he must have moved at the last minute." He felt bad.

"I swear I didn't mean to kill him."

"Well, we will let Scotland Yard handle that." Bobby surmised.

"But we still have no idea where Avery or Jack are." Tony chimed in.

"Jack must be here in London still. "Lee added.

"Yes, but the question is where? "Bobby said. "It must be somewhere in Big Al's stuff, we should look again.

"Does your brother not stay in touch with you?" Bobby asked. "I would imagine he would think you are grieving over him."

"We never had a great relationship, so I didn't think to reach out. He doesn't know I am doing this to help him. "Aaron said. He stared off into space in thought.

"Well, try now, it can't get any worse. "Bobby said patting him on the shoulder.

Aaron got out his cellphone and looked through his contact list.

"Here it is." He spoke up.

Just then, out of curiosity, Bobby asked to see his number.

"It IS him!" Bobby said.

"Who?" Luke said.

"The text I keep getting is the same number for Avery." He replied.

"Well, let's call him. We can help him." Lee jumped up.

Aaron dialed the number and let it ring numerous times. It went to voicemail, but no voice spoke, it just beeped.

"Let's see if he calls back." Luke said hopefully.

After about ten minutes of waiting for a response, there was still no reply.

"I'm going to give it a try and see if he responds to me," Bobby said.

He got out his phone and proceeded to respond to Avery's text.

"What should I reply with Dad?" he asked.

Mr. Robinson gave it some thought and replied, "Well, he most likely doesn't know Big Al is dead. We can start from there."

"Should I respond in code like he did?" He asked.

"Let's respond with something like this, "he said. As Ted paced the room he finally came up with, "*Puzzle is now missing a piece.*"

Bobby texted those words and waited for a response. After a few minutes, he got another text from an unknown number.

It read, "*St. James Square, Drinking Fountain, 7:00PM*"

Bobby showed the group the text. Excitedly they all discussed what the text means.

"It must be from Jack." Bobby said.

"I think Luke and I should meet him alone, "he started to say. "You and the rest of the group can be our spotters."

"But we still don't know what Jack looks like." Luke said. "He could tail us and spoil everything."

"Let's go back to Constable Jones. Maybe he has a picture of Jack and could help us." Bobby said.

The group all headed back to Scotland Yard and met him in his office.

"I've got a picture of Jack, but he is a master of disguise." He said.

"What about just going to the Yorkshire office?" Lee added.

"The company doesn't have a brick-and-mortar location. Nowadays most companies work remote, or they rent office space." Constable Jones said.

"Here is the last known photo, "he said, pulling out a picture.

"Wait, we saw him in the alley, remember Luke?" Bobby stood up.

"Yea, he was the guy with the clipboard." He said.

"I was the guy in the oversize coat, "Aaron confessed.

"Maybe the guy with the clipboard wanted Al and you beat him to it?"

"That's creepy, two guys with the same motive, but don't know each other." Lee chimed in.

"Well, at least we have an idea of what Jack looks like now." Bobby said.

"You think Jack is on the level wanting to meet us?" Luke asked.

"Maybe he doesn't know Al has died." Lee added.

"Well, we will have to chance it." Bobby said to the group.

"What if he has his own people with him too?" Tony spoke up.

"Constable Jones, can we get some of your men to help us, "Bobby said. "Just to be on the safe side."

"Be glad to son." He said with a smile.

After discussing the plan with the Constable, everyone headed to their rooms to relax and grab some room service.

At 6:00pm, the group met in the lobby along with men from Scotland Yard.

"How do we proceed Bobby?" One officer asked.

"Well, it's an open park, with plenty of people around so I doubt he would try anything, "he began. He opened his laptop and then opened a Google Earth snapshot of the park. "We can have people stationed in chairs near the drinking fountain as lookouts. Luke and I have a pretty good memory of what he looked like."

At 6:30pm the group got into their positions. They scattered out around the fountain and made themselves out to look like tourists. At 7:00pm, the boys made their way to the fountain. The sun was setting in the western sky and the visibility was beginning to be more challenging. Storm clouds emerged on the horizon and the boys could start to feel raindrops.

"Here he comes, "Luke motioned to Bobby.

As planned, Bobby turned to get a drink of water and ran his fingers through his hair. Both boys began small talk to make it appear as though they were in deep conversation.

Jack stopped at the drinking fountain to take a sip of water. He looked over the boys and began to make small talk.

"Where is the disc, I want it now." He whispered without moving his lips.

"Well, first, hello my name is Bobby, and this is my brother Luke." said Bobby who appeared to be annoyed at the instant demand.

"I have people watching us. And I know you also have people watching. Do not make this a scene and everything will be fine. "He demanded. "I want that disc or whoever has it. I'm not asking again."

"Big Al has it; he took it at the coffee shop." Luke said, trying out his best lie.

"Kid, I'm not stupid. I know about Big Al, now hand it over." He said, getting right in Bobby's face.

Everyone in the group was watching with intense focus. It was not going as they had planned. Suddenly, Mr. Peterson stepped forward and approached the boys.

"Let them go. I have the disc, and we can just walk away." He said, pushing between Jack and the boys. Beads of sweat started to pour down his forehead.

Jack looked hard at him and pulled a gun from his pocket.

"Move it Peterson, now!" He said boldly as he looked at the boys. "No one try and follow us."

Looking at Jack holding the gun, both boys stood frozen in their tracks.

"Take it easy, we won't do anything." Bobby said. "Doug, be careful."

Jack and Mr. Peterson slowly backed up and headed down the path. The others began rushing to the group as a pack to offer their support.

"Tell them to back off!" Jack ordered.

Bobby waved his hand to tell them to stop.

"Stop everybody, it's okay." He pleaded. "No one needs to get hurt."

The others in the park began to crowd around the group with surprised looks.

Just then, a car pulled up to the curb and Jack ordered Doug to get in the car. They headed quickly into traffic along Essex Road. The boys raced after them but soon realized the chase was futile.

"Now what?" Luke said angrily trying to catch his breath.

Bobby looked around as the others in the group joined in. He paced back and forth to formulate a plan.

"Wait a second," he told the others. He got out his phone and looked up Doug's number. "We can trace his phone."

"Really?" Luke said. "When did you do that?"

"You can punch up a number and it tracks it, if you have the App." he said.

He entered Doug's number and after a few seconds, it was aiming in on his location through cell towers.

"It's making a turn on Salop Road." He replied.

"Where is he going?" Luke said looking over his shoulder.

"It stopped." Bobby said. "I don't get it. Let's go everybody."

The boys and their father, along with Tony and Lee headed out to Essex Road and came upon a young couple unloading groceries from their SUV.

"Excuse me sir, we are in a great hurry, "Bobby said catching his breath.

"We need help getting to Salop Road, it's a matter of life and death."

The man stood frozen in surprise. He realized the looks on the faces were serious. "Okay mate, jump in. Honey, be right back."

The group all piled into the SUV and headed down Essex Road.

"Where to mate?" He said, looking at Bobby.

Bobby was looking at his phone and it kept saying Doug was stopped along Salop Road. "Where does this road lead to?" he asked.

"Look up ahead, "Luke said. "It dead ends at a river."

"I see the other car, "Tony jumped in.

The group found the abandoned car at the end of the road.

"Where did they go?" Lee asked looking around.

"They had to have gotten in some kind of boat, "Bobby said.

"What river is this and where does it lead?" Mr. Robinson asked.

"To the left it heads back to the Thames River," he said. "You head to the right it heads to back to M25 highway."

"Dad, which way should we try." Luke asked.

"My guess is they will head to the M25, "he replied. "They may have a getaway car waiting so I'll get Scotland Yard to get a helicopter en route."

Mr. Robinson picked up his phone and called headquarters. Constable Jones said he has one in the air and will work its way toward their destination. The race was on to intercept the boat before Jack and Mr. Peterson got too far away.

"How can we get back to the M25 before they do?" Luke asked.

"At this rate, with no boat of our own, we would never catch up by car. Our best option is to have the helicopter meet us," he said. "The boat can't be going that fast on a narrow river."

He called Constable Jones again.

"Meet us on Salop Road by the river. We can board the chopper and be there before they find another escape route." He said almost shouting.

The group waited for the helicopter which arrived about ten minutes later. They boarded and took off following the flow of the river. After about ten minutes of searching, they spotted the boat just getting to the M25.

"That boat was fast." Luke spoke up.

"Yes, much quicker than I had anticipated." Mr. Robinson replied.

The helicopter hovered over the river and then made a wide circle of the area.

Jack and Mr. Peterson raced from the boat, ran through the trees and up the hill where they got into a waiting car.

"I knew it!" Bobby shouted. "They have a getaway car."

The car sped away down the road and merged into traffic.

"Where do you think they are headed?" Luke asked.

"Hard to say, but they probably have some hideout." Mr. Robinson replied.

"Try his phone again just in case we lose him up here. "Luke reminded Bobby.

"Oh, right." He replied. He got out his phone and opened the App. "He's currently headed east. Let's see where the takes us".

The helicopter continued to track the car. It was headed at high speed and showing no signs of slowing down.

Bobby continued to trace Doug's phone. He was not stopping and looked to be headed towards the airport. Are they getting on a plane he thought?

"They appear to be headed to Heathrow Airport." Bobby said.

"Are you still tracking his phone?" Luke asked.

"Yes, and it's saving us a bunch of time." He replied.

"I wonder if he's doing that on purpose without Jack being aware of what you are up to." Mr. Robinson spoke up.

"Yep, he's still on M25." Bobby said excitedly.

"Yeah, but we would have no idea which flight he will get on." Luke said.

"I bet you a million to one they are headed back to the states." he said.

"Or back to the Caymans." Luke said with an eerie tone.

"Something about this says it's back home." Bobby responded.

Just then Bobby got a strange text from Doug.

It read, *Virgin #340.*

"He is helping us." Bobby said jubilantly.

"How fast can you get us to the airport?" Mr. Robinson asked the pilot.

"We can be there in ten minutes." Came the reply.

"Perfect. Boys, we can secure tickets on that flight and make sure we are in the very back of the plane, "Mr. Robinson began. "I'll contact Constable Jones when we land to let them know."

"Are we nabbing them at the airport?" Lee asked curiously.

"No, "he replied. "We need to let them lead us to where they are going."

The helicopter landed at London's Heathrow Airport a short time later.

"What about our bags at the hotel." Luke asked.

"You four get on the plane and don't lose them. I'll head back to the hotel and get all the bags and meet you at the airport. We still have time."

CHAPTER 17

GOLDEN TRAP

The boys raced to get to the terminal. They looked up at the arrivals and departures board looking for Virgin Flight 340. They spotted it and it was taking off at 10:50pm. They made their way to the ticket counter to inquire about four tickets. They noticed Washington Dulles International was on the destination board.

"Excuse me, are there any seats available on this flight?" Bobby asked.

The airline representative checked her computer screen and scanned for available seats.

"Yes, we have plenty of seats. How many would you like?" She smiled.

"Four, please. "Bobby said producing his credit card.

"Do you have any luggage to store or overhead bags?" She asked.

"Unfortunately, we left them at the hotel, but they are

being sent onto another flight." Bobby said turning almost red with embarrassment.

The ticket agent processed their tickets and boarding passes. She reminded them to have their passports available at the security gate.

The boys had been trained by their father to always have their passports with them when travelling internationally.

"Enjoy your flight." She said with a soft smile.

"Thank you." The boys said in unison.

The group made their way to the security gate and then on their way to the departure area. They noticed an open restaurant and decided to get something to eat and go over their plan.

"Let's sit inside so we can survey the crowds as they pass by without being seen." Bobby proposed.

"Especially if Jack and Mr. Peterson come strolling by." Luke added.

"We still have about two hours prior to departure, so Dad should be able to meet us here." Bobby said. He texted their father the location where they were all sitting at. The four boys all enjoyed juicy hamburgers and a plate of fries with drinks. They went over the plan once they boarded.

"We are in the very last row which works out perfectly. "Bobby began.

"With a great view if those two get on the plane, "Luke added. "Let's just make the plan work like the last time we did this."

After about an hour, they saw their father strolling down the walkway and they waved him over to their area.

"Any sign of Jack and Mr. Peterson?" Mr. Robinson asked.

"No sign yet Dad. "Luke answered. "Did you get all the bags?"

"Yes, I made sure they were tagged so they should be there waiting." he said.

Bobby looked down at this phone. He looked to see if Doug's phone was in the airport. He was in luck; it was at the main ticket counter.

"Guys, they are at the airport." Bobby said as the group gathered around.

"What's the plan once we are on the plane?" Luke asked.

"Everyone is to keep a low profile. No one is sitting behind us, so we have the advantage." he said.

"What if they spot us boarding the flight?" Tony asked. "Last row's always go first."

"Well, let's pray they aren't in first class which always goes first." Bobby replied.

"It's a long flight so we have plenty of time to map a plan once we get back home, "Mr. Robinson said. "The key will be not to lose them once we return. We need to be as discreet as possible and follow them to their destination."

After about an hour the group finished their dinner and walked into the shops to kill time before the flight. One member of the group always remained on the lookout. They finished some shopping just in time to hear the boarding call.

"All passengers on Flight #340 nonstop to Washington Dulles International Airport, please make your way to the boarding gate, "said the young flight crew member over the loudspeaker. "We will begin boarding in five minutes. All first-class passengers please make your way forward."

The boys all stopped what they were doing, and from a slight distance, watched as the passengers crowded around. There was no sign of Jack or Mr. Peterson as the initial boarding call for first class passengers had come and gone.

"Sounds like they didn't get first class." Luke told his brother nervously. "What if they end up right in front of us?"

"We'll be sunk." His brother admitted.

"Maybe this isn't their flight?" Lee chimed in, afraid to say it.

Ten minutes later the same voice came on the speaker. "Final boarding call for all first-class passengers." she said.

Suddenly two men came racing down the walkway and made their way to the counter.

It was Jack and Doug!

"Hold the plane!" Jack shouted. The men approached with their boarding passes and proceeded to get on the plane.

"They are going to recognize us." Bobby said fearfully.

"How can we get past them without being spotted?" Luke said.

"The only way to do it is to go in under some sort of disguise and hide our faces from their view." Mr. Robinson.

"But we have no idea which side of the aisle they will be on." Luke said.

"There is one way to do this." Bobby replied.

"What?" Luke said, staring at him.

"We run the risk of texting Mr. Peterson we are boarding, and he somehow distracts Jack to look out the window." He said.

"Risky move indeed." Tony said.

"I say we try it." Luke offered.

"What code do we use, in case Jack sees it?" Lee asked.

Bobby thought for a moment and looked around the terminal for any type of inspiration. He noticed another flight boarding and large crowds had started to gather.

"Let's be the last of the passengers in our rows," he said. "We will use code based on someone in front of us."

The young lady at the ticket counter picked up the microphone.

"Now boarding Flight 340 non-stop service to Washington

Dulles International Airport. We will be boarding rows 30-39." she said.

The boys purposefully got their stuff together slowly. Bobby had purchased a small backpack in the outlet stores and loaded it with water and snacks.

Bobby noticed a small child travelling with their parents. He was carrying a small teddy bear. That's the code Bobby thought! They will get behind them when they board the plane.

Bobby got out his phone and texted to Doug with the simple code words: Teddy Bear

Let's hope he sees it and distracts Jack, he thought. They got in behind the building crowd of passengers gathered in front of the door leading down to the entrance of the plane. They had to make sure they got behind the family with the small child or the plan would be ruined.

Suddenly the small child tugged on his mother's coat.

"I have to use the bathroom," he pleaded to his mother.

Bobby and Luke froze with fear. They can't have him miss the flight.

"As soon as we are on board sweetie, we will use the bathroom. We are almost there." She promised, looking into his eyes.

The group got closer and closer to the door as the boys and their father moved in right behind them. Bobby scanned the area to make sure no one else might disrupt their plans.

The ticket agent took their boarding passes, and they travelled down the gangway to the plane. Bobby's phone received no response text back from Doug. His fears heightened that he would not look at his phone in time.

They got closer to the door of the plane when Bobby's phone suddenly sounded the text alert.

All he received was a smiley face emoji.

Bobby let out a huge sigh of relief and showed Luke his phone. He looked at the others with an expression of satisfaction. The question remained? Which side of the plane was Doug going to be on? Bobby totally forgot to ask that question and shook his head in disappointment at himself.

They boarded the plane slowly and from behind other passengers both boys scanned the passengers. Bobby agreed to look left, and Luke said that he would look to the right.

Bingo!

Bobby spotted Doug and Jack looking out the side of the plane. The boys had to make sure they rushed it along just in case Jack turned back to the aisle.

They had all just passed Jack sitting in the aisle with seconds to spare as he looked back at the incoming passengers. The group made it to the rear of the plane and situated themselves in their seats. After all the passengers were on board, and the airline crew did their pre-flight check, the plane backed away from the gate. Less than ten minutes later the flight was airborne.

The boys sat side by side next to their father and discussed the case from all angles and pitched ideas back and forth to each other on how to entrap Jack to admitting guilt. They concluded that Mr. Peterson was going to be the key to getting Jack to confess to kidnapping and racketeering.

"We also to need to solve the whole mystery of that safe at Sky Mountain." Luke added. "Getting into the disk is crucial."

The flight was long, and the group were very tired upon landing at Dulles. It was a cold, rainy day indicative of their moods and did not raise their spirits. They had one focus at hand and that was to trail Jack and Doug to see where they would end up.

"He is going to get off the plane first and we can't afford to lose them now." Luke said worried.

"Well, they must go through customs and then onto the baggage claim area so that will at least slow them down some." Bobby said to his brother with a cheerful smile.

After exiting the plane, the passengers all made their way to the customs area. The room was crowded with people all coming in from the other international flights.

The group kept pace with Jack and Doug. After clearing customs, they headed to the baggage claim area. The boys were cautious to keep their distance and observe Jack from afar.

They collected their bags and made their way down the ramp to the arrival door. They hurried outside and got into a Washington Flyer taxi and merged into traffic.

"They couldn't have spotted us." Bobby shouted hurrying to the door.

The group all headed for Washington Flyer taxis and quickly loaded their bags into the trunk.

"Bobby, you and Tony go down the Dulles Toll Road. If you see them give us a call." Mr. Robinson said hurriedly.

"Where will you three go?" Bobby shot back.

"There are only two options out of the airport. We will head down Route 28 and see if we can catch them that way. One of us should be able to catch up to them in short time." He replied.

The boys got in their taxis and proceeded to head out. Traffic around the airports' arrivals circle was almost at a standstill. Car horns were honking, and everyone was jockeying to get into position to head for the exit. The driver weaved his way around cars lined up loading passengers.

"Driver, we are in a hurry, could you get us to the toll road quickly? We would certainly make it worth your while." Bobby said frantically.

The driver looked at his passengers in the rearview mirror

with skepticism. He would not break any speed rules, but sensed they were telling the truth.

Meanwhile, Mr. Robinson and the others gathered speed and made the exit off onto Route 28. They did not immediately see the other car. At once they spotted the car in the left lane and Mr. Robinson asked the driver to catch up to them.

"That's Saeed's car ahead of us." The driver responded.

"Can you ask him discreetly the intended destination without tipping off the passengers?" He asked.

The driver got on the radio and asked in his native language where he was taking the passengers. He got his response and advised the group.

"Perfect, he's going to Middleburg. I will call Bobby and let him know."

"Turn around and head to the Salamander Resort in Middleburg." He told his eldest son. "We will meet you at the Red Fox Inn just down the street."

Thirty minutes later the group met in the lobby and discussed the next steps.

"I wonder why they chose that place?" Luke asked.

"Looks like there is a big event in town this weekend. The streets are crowded with tourists." Bobby said.

"This Saturday is the annual Gold Cup race." Mr. Robinson replied pointing to a sign by the front desk. "We would need to get tickets to this, and I know just the person to call to help us out. We can setup by the fence and blend right in."

He placed a call to a former colleague to happened to live out here in Middleburg and attended every year. The last couple of years due to the pandemic the events had been canceled.

"Sam, it's Ted Robinson. Fine, how are Brenda and the kids?" He spoke for a little while to catch up on old times. "Got a favor to ask of you." He filled him in on all the details up to this point. With a smile on his face, the boys knew the answer.

"Thanks Sam, we will see you on Saturday. Let us know what we can bring." He hung up the phone. "All set, they have a spot by the fence, and we can scope the area and see if we see Jack and Doug." He replied.

The group was able to get two rooms at the Middleburg Inn due to some last-minute cancellations. They unpacked their bags and decided to walk the streets to get a bit of fresh air and relax. They found outdoor seats at the Main Street Oyster Bar across the street from the hotel. From this vantage point they could see if Jack and Doug happened to walk down the street. The meal was finished about an hour later and no one spotted the duo.

"How do we know where to meet Sam?" Bobby asked his father.

"He gave me directions. It's just up the road on the left about fifteen minutes away.

They do this every year and have a spot by the fence." He replied.

The next day they met up with Sam and his family and introductions were made to everyone. A skirted table had been set out with a big bouquet of flowers set up in the middle. Three chafing dishes had been set out with mini crab cakes and scallops with bacon. A feast fit for a king was enjoyed by all those in attendance. After everyone settled in, Ted and Sam got two seats by the fence so he could bring Sam up to speed on the reason for their joining the group.

"Sounds like a mystery for James Bond." Sam laughed patting his friend on the shoulder.

The races began and the crowd noise increased as the competition between the horses and their riders sped by the sound of the roaring crowds. During the races the boys and their friends discussed the case from all angles and tossed out ideas on how to capture Jack. All agreed that they needed to do all they could do to help Mr. Peterson. They concluded that Jack must have the disk and is holding Doug as hostage to make a sale of the disk to a third party here at the races.

"This means there's one thing that we have to do," Bobby said. "We must find those two somehow and that disk."

"How do we do that?" Lee asked.

Bobby looked around for binoculars. He deduced that someone in the group must have brought a pair to the races. He looked in all the cars and found a pair in the back seat. He got them out and walked to the railing. He looked all up the hill along the railing to scan the crowd. After another round of looking, he came across a group that looked suspicious. He focused the binoculars and saw Doug standing by the railing looking at a racing program.

Bobby shouted, "I found him!" He gave the binoculars to Luke and asked him to look at about thirty yards up on the left. Luke saw him and concurred with Bobby on his find. They talked things over with their father as to how they should approach their next move.

Bobby suggested to Luke, "Let's take a walk up there."

"Maybe we will spot Doug and he will know we are here to help him get out of this situation." Luke agreed.

They told their father that they and the boys would take a walk up the road and be back in about fifteen minutes, then set off. The boys walked up slowly passing the cars and scanning the patrons at the railings.

"We need to be careful, "Bobby warned the group. "We don't know who else is here."

Suddenly Luke grabbed his brother's arm. "I just had an idea. Maybe Big Al on his deathbed confessed that Jack was behind it all and its written down somewhere."

"You mean he was really innocent?" Tony asked.

"Not totally, "Luke replied, "At some point in every mystery, someone who seems like the real suspect, really isn't guilty."

As they walked on, all the boys scanned the area to spot Jack. He was nowhere to be found.

"Maybe Jack is sitting in a chair, and we can't spot him." Luke said.

They walked up cautiously and got near the row of cars that shielded the group from the fence. Bobby spotted Doug, who was still looking at his race programs. He didn't recognize anyone else in the group. The attendees all appeared to be in their late 30's with an even mix of ladies to men. The ladies were dressed in fancy styles wearing bright colored big, brimmed hats that were a signature of the horse racing community. They decided to walk up further and see if they could get a better advantage point looking back at the group.

Bobby decided to send a text to Doug to see if he would respond but was unsure what emoji to send. He then quickly thought of a horse emoji. He sent it and waited for a reply all the while looking right at Doug from behind a row of cars.

When Doug didn't reach for his phone right away Bobby was unsure the text had gone through. He looked at his phone and the confidence drained from his face.

"Not delivered!" the message read in bright red letters.

Bobby grew frustrated but realized they were in an area that did not have good cell coverage and probably, if it did, everyone was using up the bandwidth. He got a sudden ping on his phone. Success!

He told Luke and the others that it had gone through, and they looked in Doug's direction. He looked straight at them, but for fear of giving away his position, acted like he didn't see them and turned to talk with the others in the group.

Suddenly, cheers went up as the thundering sound of hooves approached the area and the horses raced by the fences in a sudden act of fury. The boys became momentarily mesmerized at the scene and followed the horses as they raced by.

Bobby turned to Luke and standing right there was Jack Grisham.

"Okay kid, you and your friends, move it." He glared at him.

He was holding a gun in his hand.

CHAPTER 18

STARTLING DISCOVERY

Realizing they had been caught off guard, the boys were led to the group standing by the fence.

"Make a move and it will be your last." He calmly warned them.

"Everyone, we have some guests who would like to join us for the last race of the day." Jack announced to the group in a creepy sounding voice. Doug looked at Bobby and then immediately to Jack. He showed no emotion and went along with the plan.

"Let me introduce you boys to a few friends of mine, "he said in a menacing tone." He went around the group and the boys immediately recognized three individuals who they had met in the fifth-floor office the day they had been gassed. The group all had a robotic look on their faces as if they were programmed to show no emotions. After the race had ended, Jack turned to two of his beefy guards and motioned them to a waiting car with the boys and gave them instructions.

"Take these annoying little fleas to the house and wait for my further instructions." Jack ordered.

Doug came running up to the group and asked what Jack's plan was going to be.

"I think you should be worried what we are going to do with you." He replied, his eyes turning an evil shape. "You don't produce that login like I had warned you, and it will be your final mistake."

During this whole time, Bobby had wondered about one man who was standing with the group but looked completely out of place. He didn't recognize him at all.

"Take him with you." He shoved Doug into his bodyguard.

The boys and Doug were all piled into waiting SUV's. Jack returned to the group and told them the time had come.

The group left everything by the fence and proceeded to get into their cars and spun the tires in the dirt to make a quick exit.

"What should we do with these bratty kids?" said one of the bodyguards.

"We first need to get that stupid disk to work." A visibly frustrated Jack looked at Doug. He looked out the window as light rain began to fall. He turned back to Doug, and with a stare as cold as the rain outside, gave him one last chance.

"Get us into that disk, or the boys have had it." He said.

"Jack, there is no need to hurt anyone. Please let the boys go and I'll promise as soon as we get to the office, I will make it happen." He pleaded.

"Shut up!" He screamed. "These dumb kids don't need to know our plan."

Bobby whispered to Luke, "Now I know where I saw those three. They were with that company Anderson CPA, remember?

Luke looked back at Bobby and said, "You're right."

"Both of you shut up. You won't be knowing anymore of our plans so you both might as well just sit quietly." One of the bodyguards snarled.

Thirty minutes later they arrived back at the office building where they interned. They waited in the car as Doug and Jack proceeded into the building. They returned a short time later and the boys noticed a different tone with Jack. He had an evil smile on his face.

"Got what we need, let's go." He ordered the driver.

"Where are you taking us?" Bobby demanded.

"We are taking a little drive out into the country." Jack stared at them.

"Jack, you promised you'd let them go if I gave you the code. Please, there is no need to keep them." Doug said.

"I will say when they are let go." Jack shouted.

An hour later the cars exited the highway just off Route 29 and headed down a long and winding country road. They came into a small town that looked to be abandoned. They proceeded down the main street and turned suddenly into an old gas station that had two large bay doors. Suddenly a garage door opened, and the cars vanished from view.

The boys were ushered from the car with guns aimed at them and strong armed into the back of the gas station. They entered through a door and made their way down a long set of steps to a dimly lit hallway.

They proceeded about twenty yards and made their way up another set of steps into an abandoned house. They were pushed into a darkened back bedroom and tied up on cots. The door was closed, and the group of men made their way to an adjoining room. The boys strained to hear the conversation in the next room.

"The plan is working and soon we will have all the data we need to finally complete the sale to Rota-Vonni. Nobody has any clue what we've done. "Jack snarled as he paced the room. "That fool Avery is confirmed to be out of the picture now that those snooping kids found the plane and his corpse in it."

"Well, with Big Al out of the picture as well boss, it's all yours." Said one of the husky bodyguards.

"I now own two companies, more for me." He laughed out loud.

"When are we meeting with Rota-Vonni boss?" Another guard asked.

"Good question, let me find out where they are." Jack replied. "Our friends with Anderson will meet us as well and we get out of this town and head south to figure out who to takeover next."

Jack got his cell out of his pocket and placed a call. He went outside so no one could hear what he was saying. After about ten minutes he came back into the house and headed for the room where the boys were sitting all tied up.

"Such a shame, "Jack began as he eyed the boys, "that you both just couldn't stay out of my way. All your investigative work is going to get you both nowhere. No one knows you're here and by the time they do figure it out, we will be in South America." His eyes glared at them.

Jack got right up into their faces, flashed the disk in front of them, and let out an ear-splitting laugh. "You little punks! You caused more trouble than was necessary, and now you'll suffer some pain."

Jack's cellphone rang and he went to answer it. "We are at that old gas station down on Main Street. It's called Sunny's Gas Station. My men will open the bay doors when you get here." He replied. "This town has hardly anybody in it, and no one pays any attention. Hurry up." He barked.

He turned to his men and told them to pack up everything and be ready to move out in fifteen minutes. They left the room and locked the door behind them, leaving the boys to themselves.

Bobby turned to Luke as they sat on the cots against the wall and tried to wriggle his hands free. He positioned himself against Luke's back to try and untie the ropes binding their wrists. It was no use and they both tried to position themselves with their backs against the wall.

"You think Dad saw us get into those cars?" Bobby asked the others.

"He might have, but everything went by so fast." Luke answered.

Tony and Lee did the same and sat back-to-back to try and wriggle their hands free. The faint sound of the garage bay doors opening indicated that the group was heading out.

"They really are leaving us here." Lee said in a frightened tone.

"We have our cellphones remember. They must have forgotten to take those since they were in such a hurry. I'm sure our numbers can be traced to this location somehow." Luke said, trying to be cheerful. Tony noticed some broken furniture across the room. A few splintered tables and chairs sat in the corner.

"Everyone try and work your way across the room. We can use the sharp ends of those chairs." He replied.

"Luke and I are going to try and see if there is a sharp part of this cot and wedge our ropes in there." Bobby said. After about ten minutes their ropes snapped free.

"Got it!" Luke shouted.

"Keep it down. They may have let someone behind." Bobby said, trying to whisper.

The boys crept silently up to the bedroom door. Bobby pressed his ear against it but could not make out any sounds on the other side. He quietly opened the door just slightly and looked down the hallway. He couldn't see anyone gathered in the main room. The house was one level and looked to have been built back in the 1960's. It was obvious no one had lived in the home for quite a while and had been a hideout. Graffiti was marked up all down the hallway with proof that young kids must have also made it a playground. The room they were currently in was a guest bedroom at one point due to its rather overall small size.

Bobby looked to his right and crept slowly down the hallway to the master bedroom just to be sure they would not be caught by surprise. All the boys had mastered using hand signals when doing sleuthing work. The group all stuck together and made their way down the hall to the living room area, being very careful not to make any sounds. The aging house had creaky floors, so the group proceeded at a snail's pace.

Bobby whispered to Luke, "They must be outside. I can hear faint sounds coming from the garage area."

Luke nodded in agreement, and they crouched low and made it to the kitchen entrance. From just outside earshot, Bobby could hear Jack talking in an excited tone. He raised his head slightly and could see six men that were standing in the yard between the gas station and the house. The SUV's were parked in the bays facing outward this time.

"Get the bags and the equipment all loaded up into the cars. We need to get everything out of here and leave no traces behind, "he said. "The rest of the gear is at the cabin at Sky Mountain. I still want to find that person that tried to remove that safe from the house. And when I do, they've had it."

"You think old man Johnson and his son, did it?" one man asked.

"Not sure, but glad they caught those stupid kids when

they did. Otherwise, it would have blown our operation sky high."

"Boss, what if those kids escape?" One man asked.

"If they do, which won't be for a while, they have no idea of our plans. We will be to the house and out of there before any cops know of our plan." Jack replied as he was texting on his phone. Just before everything was wrapped up, Jack turned to Doug and had him handcuffed.

"Jack, you double-crosser. I got you everything you needed. You can't turn on me like this." Doug said his face turned beat red.

Jack got up in Doug's face with an icy cold stare. "I could have dropped you in the river once you got me into the disk. But now that I have you as my prisoner, I have bigger plans for you after you do me one more favor."

Soon, the SUV's were brought out from the garage and Doug noticed they had been painted.

"Everything's loaded boss." one man said.

The men loaded up and closed the bay doors. They proceeded out to the main street and turned left onto the country road. The sound of tires began to fade into the distance.

The boys all proceeded cautiously to the kitchen and looked all around to make sure no one was left. They opened the door and walked across to the garage and peeked in. Nothing was left of Jack and his henchmen except a rack of gallons of paint. On the floor in a pile were old license plates.

"The must have painted the cars and switched license plates." Luke said.

Bobby went to open the cans and noticed they were all a dark shade of blue. "They must have done this color to just slightly throw off anyone who would be looking for a black SUV." He said, turning to the group.

Bobby looked down at his cellphone and noticed he had only one bar of energy left on his battery.

"What town are we even in?" Luke asked looking around.

"Your guess is as good as mine, "Bobby began. "But we need to find someone here who can help us." The group walked out onto main street and looked in both directions.

The group split up and walked down both sides of the street in search of anyone who could help. Bobby and Lee walked down the left side and investigated abandoned shops looking for any signs of life. Luke and Tony walked down the right side of the street and made a right turn and immediately found an old man loading supplies into his truck.

"Excuse me sir, "Luke politely asked.

The man turned and gave them a look of annoyance. He turned back and continued to load materials into his truck. Luke was getting annoyed at the impolite gesture.

"We would just like to ask what town we are in?" Luke asked again.

The man turned around again and whispered in soft tone, "This is the town of Upperville." He squinted his eyes at the boys.

"We mean no harm sir. We were held captive in Sunny's Gas Station and trying to find out if some SUV's happened this way." Tony said pleasantly.

The other old man continued to eye them suspiciously. After looking them over some more, he softened his tone.

"The names Grayson, "he said, extending his hand.

The boys explained the whole story to Grayson beginning with the races that took place in Middleburg.

"Does everyone in town go to these races? The place is empty." Luke said.

"You must not be from here young man, "he said. "These races have been going on for over a century. It is the one big event of the year next to the Middleburg Hunt Races at Christmas time. When these events take place the town empties out like grocery stores in a snowstorm."

"That explains why they took us away so fast, "Tony said. "To make sure no one would be around to see them."

By this time Bobby and Lee had joined the group and they introduced them to Grayson. They asked him how long Sunny's had been closed.

"That place gives me the creeps. It has been abandoned for a long time. Not too long ago these fellas came driving around town looking suspicious and all."

"Tell us more Grayson, it might help our case." Bobby pleaded.

"Well, old man Winters owned the house and gas station, "he began. "He died about ten years ago and there was no will. The house and gas station had just gone empty. These fellas came into town claiming to be long lost relatives and would be fixing it up to put it on the market. No one here in town had any reason to doubt them. Then one night me and the wife were walking down Main Street and heard strange sounds coming from the garage. We peeked around the corner and saw one light coming from the garage. It didn't look like they were fixing up the house. Two men come out and began arguing and next thing we know one of them was shot dead."

"What happened to the other man who got shot?" Luke asked excitedly.

"We turned around and left and didn't want to know anything about it."

"Did the police show up?" Bobby asked.

"They sure did, but there was no evidence to be had, so they let the case go." Grayson responded.

"There had to be blood on the ground." Lee protested.

"Nothing, I'm telling you. They looked all around and not one drop was to be had."

"Did you ever see that man again?" Luke asked.

"We surely did not. It was as if nothing had happened." he said.

"Does the station still have working pumps?" Bobby inquired.

"They haven't worked in years. Folks use the gas station down the road a ways now." he said. "We did see a lot of cars go in the bays to be painted, so they must have had a body shop. But no one lived in the house best we could tell."

Out of the corner of his eye, Luke could see a man coming down the side road. He was swaying back and forth and looked to be in a great deal of pain.

"Doug!" Luke shouted.

They all rushed to Doug's side as he appeared to have bumps and bruises, and a gash on his head.

"What happened?" Bobby asked with a concerned look on his face.

"Well, we got on the road, and I pleaded with Jack not to harm me. I was stupid to get him into that disk, but what choice did I have?" He pleaded as he bent over in pain."

"Who were all those people with him?" Luke implored.

"Those are all his co-conspirators. I truly don't think some of them know the real reason he is getting a strangle hold and owning these companies." He added.

"What do you mean?" Bobby asked perplexed.

"They all think it's a legit business move. He is really in deals with some group in South America to develop software to crash computer systems." he said.

"So, it's a malware software?" Lance offered.

"Exactly, but it's so sophisticated that it would take a really smart tech to figure out how to counteract it." He replied.

"We recognized three people at the races who were with a setup fake accounting firm." Bobby said.

"It's not a fake company, Bobby, it's legit. They are in cahoots with Jack to gain all they can." He replied.

"Well, who then was the other guy? He looked totally out of place with this group." Luke added.

"You know, I was asking myself the same thing. Maybe he's one of Jack's co-owners. He did seem to be just taking it all in."

CHAPTER 19

TRAPPED

"We have to get out of here and find out where they are" Luke said, looking around at the town. "Dad doesn't know where we are."

"And cell service isn't the greatest." Bobby added.

Grayson offered to take a group up to the races while the others remained in town.

"That would be great, thanks so much." Bobby smiled.

Bobby and Luke got into Grayson's truck, and they headed down route 50 to the racetrack. As they got closer, they could see the crowds start to exit the race. They pulled into the main driveway and made their way up the road.

"Where was your group located at?" Grayson asked.

"Just up ahead on the right." Bobby replied.

The truck slowly made its way up further and suddenly the boys noticed their father on the phone with a group of people.

"Stop right here!" Luke said.

Their father noticed them and ended his call. The boys jumped out greeted their father warmly.

"Boys, what happened?" he said giving them each a hug.

"Long story Dad, but Jack got away." Bobby said.

He proceeded to tell their father all that had happened since they were taken from the track. He ended up discovering Doug coming down the road in pain.

"What's our next move?" Bobby asked.

"Well, the sense is Jack is headed back to Sky Mountain to some hideout and will clear it out. But where that is now is a mystery." He replied.

"And we don't have Doug's phone to track him." Luke said dejected.

Mr. Robinson paced back and forth for a few minutes while the boys thanked Grayson for the help.

"Anytime boys. I'll head back and tell the others and we will be back in just a little while." He said smiling and gave a wave goodbye.

They turned back to their father, and they all sat in the chairs by the fence coming up with a plan.

"Dad, Luke and I are curious about one person in the group who we didn't recognize." Bobby said.

"Who was that?" His father shot back.

"Tall gentleman, wore glasses and had an English attire." Luke said.

"I do remember seeing someone like that, but it's a mystery to me as well." he replied.

"We think he's Jack's right hand man." Bobby remarked.

"Let's start with where you saw the safe." Mr. Robinson said. "You boys say you saw that sitting all by itself, right?"

"Yes, that first night and then we got knocked cold." Bobby said.

"You remember where that area is?" he replied.

Bobby got out his phone and searched for his history of calls. "Got it. It's just west of here, about an hour's drive."

"Great, let's head back to the house and grab some gear. We can scope out the area tonight. The weather should be clear." Mr. Robinson said.

The group met back at the Robinson home to map out the details. The sun was starting to set when the group of six made their way down Route 29.

They made their way up and over the mountain roads and came to the same spot they had seen the safe. Google Maps had indicated this was close to Crooked Creek Run.

It was totally dark when the group hid the cars in a batch of bushes by the river. They agreed to follow the river with small canoes to see where the river led them to. Not far up the river they came across a two-story house off to the right. There was a light on in the upstairs room.

"Do you think this is their hideout?" Luke whispered to Bobby.

"One way to find out." his brother remarked.

"What I can't figure out is why here? Why this location?" Tony inquired.

"I agree. There has to be some logical explanation." Lee chimed in.

"It could be they just wanted some far-out remote location so they wouldn't be suspected at all." Bobby said.

They kept their voices low and continued to watch the house.

"Or this could be that old man's house, remember." Luke said looking at his brother.

"True, but we've come this far not to find out." He replied.

Disembarking from the boats, they quietly made their way to the side of the house. Mr. Robinson got out his night vision googles and scanned the area.

"I see two guards just outside the side door, "he whispered. "They both have guns in their hands. It would be too dangerous to approach them."

He continued to survey the outside of the house for more guards. He couldn't see anymore. As he raised his goggles, he could see one man standing in the window. "I see Jack boys, and he looks to be upset by something."

"We must get closer to see if we can spot anything." Bobby said.

"Let's split up and surround the house." Luke replied.

Mr. Robinson would go with Luke and Tony. Bobby, Doug, and Lee would take the other side of the house.

"How will we signal you?" Bobby said. "I don't want the light of our phones to give us away."

Mr. Robinson thought for a moment. He remembered back in his agent days where the group would use ordinary sounds as an indicator of position so as not to give away their positions.

"I'm going to do a particular bird call in morse code. Listen for this sound. He demonstrated in a very low volume and placed it next to Bobby's ear. "When you hear it then you will know it's me. Even sounds means I'm on the side of the house and odd sounds will mean I'm on the end of the house."

The groups split up and Bobby, Doug and Lee kneeled below the bushes and went around the house towards the driveway. Mr. Robinson and his group made their way along the riverbank. Mr. Robinson spotted two more guards by the back door of the house. That makes four guards on the outside, he thought. When they got to their spot they kneeled down and watched the house. He waited for a few minutes for the boys to get in position by the driveway. He proceeded to give three loud bird calls in code.

"How will we know they got the bird calls Dad? Luke asked.

"I told Bobby one same loud bird call meant they received it." He replied.

They waited for the bird call to sound, and none came. Mr. Robinson started to get a little worried when suddenly, they heard the sound.

"He's in position." He whispered.

The old two-story house stood tall and quiet against the nighttime sky. A galaxy of brightly lit stars stretched across the horizon. The moon, off in the distance, hovered big and bright like the color of butter. Silently, Bobby and the others tiptoed up to the side of the house. He sounded out four bird calls indicating his position. He heard back one bird sound that his call was received.

Bobby slowly slid to a ground floor window and peered in. It was dark and he could not make out any movement. The others were standing by his side looking in both directions for any sign of the guards. He tried the window, and it was locked. He gently moved to the next window and noticed it too was also locked. He noticed next to him a double cellar door.

"This must be how they got into the house." He thought to himself.

He tried the door and slowly raised it up hoping not to make any creaking sounds. "It works!" He whispered to the others.

"Hurry up." Lee whispered back.

Quickly and quietly the group descended the stairs into darkness and closed the door above them. They hesitated to turn on their cellphone flashlights and have them light up the room. Lee turned his on and partly covered with his hand to offer a little light in the room. It had a musty, dry smell to it.

As they looked around the room, they noticed it was an old sawmill full of sawhorses and firewood.

"This house must date back to the early part of the 19th century." Lee whispered to Doug. He nodded in agreement. At the far end of the room, they noticed a wooden set of stairs leading to the main level of the house. The others turned on their cellphone lights and did the same. They walked slowly around the room to get their bearings. They could hear sounds coming from above and froze in their tracks.

"This was perfectly planned but it is being run with idiotic incompetence," Jack shouted. "Those stupid kids are ruining this. If they escaped, I will have all of your heads for this."

As they approached the stairs, they heard footsteps behind them.

"Freeze!"

Bobby turned around to see two armed guards pointing their weapons at them. Confronted with capture, the group put their hands over their heads while holding their cellphones.

"We'll take those. You won't be needing them anymore." One man said with an evil tone in his voice. "Move it."

The group was muscled up the stairs and through the door in the front hallway. The prisoners were taken into the large living room area and had their hands tied behind their backs. They sat in wooden chairs next to the fireplace and had guns trained on them.

A double door was opened that led into an adjoining room and Jack appeared in the doorway along with two other men. One of the men was the same one they saw at the horse races.

"Well, if it isn't the Robinsons. You fools escaped one house, but I assure you that you won't be leaving this one." He gave a cold, hard stare at Bobby. "Your visit here causes me tremendous inconvenience but won't stop my plans." Jack's eyes appeared to sparkle with hate.

The stranger stepped forward and took hold of Jack's arm and guided him off to the side.

"Let's just get the sale done to Rota-Vonni and get out of here." He pleaded with him. "Once we do that, clear our stuff out of here and off to South America where no one will be able to catch us. They don't know anything about our operation."

Jack swung the stranger's arm away and rage started to build up in him as he paced the room.

"These kids know too much already." He screamed. "I'm not going to have it blow up in our faces."

"Exactly, let's do what we need to do." he said calmly. "Make the final sale and let's get out of here."

"Get the cars ready to load up. We leave out of Annapolis tonight on the private yacht." He barked his orders to his men.

They proceeded to walk into the kitchen area where they had their computers set up.

While Bobby, Doug and Lee were tied up on wooden chairs, Jack and his partner sat around the kitchen table in a heated conversation.

"I want one hundred million for all the data we have on that company Pioneer Corporation," Jack said. He was on his cellphone and had the speaker on.

"How do we know you won't double-cross us, Jack?" came the strange voice on the other end.

"Once I have confirmation that the money is in my Cayman Islands account, I will give you a login and you can create your new passwords, and this ends our little transaction." He said coldly. "All we want is the money and it's all yours to do whatever nasty deeds your heart's desire."

Bobby could see from his vantage point into the kitchen. The strange man was sitting across from Jack. He had his cellphone under the table and looked to be texting someone. Was he the double crosser, Bobby wondered.

Lee leaned into Bobby and said, "Where's the cavalry? Your Dad must know something went wrong, right?" He looked into Bobby's eyes.

Bobby whispered back to Lee, "Dad must have contacted the police by now and they are on the way."

"Done. Let's move out." Jack ordered.

"Jack, I haven't received the new login." the man on the phone said in a high pitch voice.

"I sent it to you, that's your problem." He replied angrily.

He hung up the phone. The men began to gather up the computers and put them in silver cases. The strange man took one of the silver cases himself and proceeded out the door.

"What do we do with them Jack?" said one of the guards.

"The timer on the bombs started the minute I had confirmation of the money in my account, "he replied smoothly. "The house won't exist in about thirty minutes, which gives us plenty of time to get a head start."

Jack approached the boys and Doug and stared at them for a good thirty seconds.

"Jack, it was you and Big Al all along that stole from Pioneer." Doug spoke up.

Jack glared at Doug. "Avery was a fool not to sell to me when I wanted to purchase his company. I knew Big Al had an ingenious plan to try to ruin Avery's company when he stole the logistics plans. I went to college with Greg Gaines, and he never partnered with me. After he died about ten years ago I vowed to get revenge on him one day, and that day is now."

Doug replied, "So Big Al was just a pawn in your plan."

"Big Al was stupid. He tried to get too big for his own good and I needed to get him out of the way," Jack shot back. "He fell for all my charm, and I sold his company and now selling Pioneer makes me even richer."

"You don't care that Big Al was killed?" Lee asked.

"Why should I, more for me, and less for you." Jack laughed.

Jack and his guards went back into the kitchen and met with the other man to finalize plans to evacuate.

Bobby whispered to Lee, "We need to keep Jack talking till Luke and the police can get here. It's our last chance."

"I still can't figure out who the other man is." Doug said perplexed.

"One would hope he's outfoxing Jack." Lee said in a hopeful tone.

The prisoners were all led down the stairwell into the basement and tied up with their backs behind the chairs.

Bobby tried to keep Jack talking. "Since this is our last opportunity to chat, why did Greg Gaines keep you out? I mean it's obvious. "Bobby said.

"I don't mind telling you, "Jack grinned. "Greg knew I had the better brains for the operation but didn't like my methods of how I went about getting what I wanted. I have always gotten what I wanted. He chose to work with that idiot Avery Turnpike. And now, the tables have turned."

"Jack, let's go." The strange man said.

"Better luck in your next life boys." Jack said with a laugh.

"Jack, you can't leave me here with them. I got you what you wanted."

Doug screamed at him, rocking violently back and forth in his chair.

Jack turned to Doug and said, "I'm the King, and you are the pawn."

The men turned and walked up the stairs and locked the door. The boys could hear footsteps above them.

Suddenly, a shot rang out and startled the group.

"What the heck was that?" A startled Lee said to the group.

"Maybe somebody shot Jack and double crossed him." Bobby replied.

Soon the group heard shouts and loud footsteps above. Tables and chairs were being overturned and rustling sounds indicated chaos had ensued.

"Everybody clear out. Now!" Jack shouted.

The sounds became louder and finally the boys heard a door slam. Suddenly there was complete silence. Bobby looked all around for signs of the bomb they had planted in the basement. He noticed in the corner of the basement red digital lights.

"Everybody look over there!" he said, motioning with his eyes.

"Jack wasn't kidding Bobby! We only have fifteen minutes." Lee echoed.

Soon the basement door opened, and the boys could hear someone coming down the stairs slowly. At the same time, they heard the front door upstairs get kicked in and footsteps racing along the floor. The light was turned on and the other man that was with Jack had crumbled to the bottom of the stairs.

He had been shot.

Bobby saw his father, Luke and Tony come right behind him. Mr. Robinson helped the man to his feet and guided him to a chair.

"He's been shot in the shoulder." Mr. Robinson declared. He looked all around for something to stop the bleeding. He found some old tee shirts in a box in the corner of the room. He ripped one in two and applied them to the man's shoulder as a tourniquet.

"What happened?" Bobby and Mr. Robinson said in unison.

"You go first." Mr. Robinson smiled at his son.

"Jack told us everything, but we have to get out of here

quickly." He said, pointing to the bomb in the corner. I'll tell you more when we get outside."

As they quickly exited the house, Bobby explained all that had happened when they attempted to sneak in the cellar door.

"We heard all of them talking above us but had not heard Jack's henchmen sneak up behind us." he said out of breath.

"Jack's planning to head to Annapolis and take a secret yacht out onto Chesapeake Bay and head south." Doug chimed in.

"We need to find him and stop him." Bobby said.

"Jack admitted everything to us. He's convinced he is untouchable. He's taking all his money and headed to South America."

BOOM!

The force of the blast from the house sent everyone running for cover. Soon the house was engulfed in flames. Sirens could be heard in the distance and the red flashing lights became brighter and brighter.

"That was close." Luke said. He was shaking from the effects of the blast.

"We must get this man to a hospital." Mr. Robinson announced.

"I'll be alright Ted." Avery replied.

The boys all turned to him with a look of shock on their faces.

"Dad, who is this?" Bobby asked.

Mr. Robinson couldn't hide his secret anymore. Avery had accidentally spoken too soon.

"Boys, I would like you to meet Avery Turnpike." He announced smiling.

Bobby and Luke's jaws dropped.

"I've been the one tricking Jack this whole time," Avery said, holding his shoulder.

"It's a long story. You see, Jack and I had never met before. I knew someone was trying to ruin the company, so I hired your dad about six years ago. We have been after Big Al and Jack all this time. About a year later I found out through some of Greg's old papers that someone had stolen his plans, but we couldn't find them. Then strange calls started coming in to try and blackmail us to sell. We went under cover, and I faked my death to throw them off their plans. I had to hide out and work with Ted to solve this case.

"Wait a second, "Bobby interrupted. "Who was the man on the call with Jack at the house?"

"My brother Aaron." Avery replied. "He's been in on this all along. We wanted to double cross Jack and beat him at his own game. That was me you saw texting to him under the table."

The police and the fire department finally showed up. The house fire was put under control and Avery had his shoulder all patched up.

"Boys, we have to find Jack and stop him." Ted finally said.

"Where do we start, he's got to be long gone by now?." Bobby said.

"Wait a second. Didn't he say he was heading out of Annapolis?" Lee asked.

"He is and I think I know where that yacht is." Avery said.

Mr. Robinson got on the phone with the authorities and briefed them on what had happened at the house.

"When we know more Frank, I'll be in touch. We are headed for the marina now and will commandeer a houseboat and stay out of sight." he said.

"Let's go everybody." Ted said helping Avery to a waiting SUV.

CHAPTER 20

CAPTURED

About two hours later they arrived at the waterfront. They drove around in the tinted window SUV so as not to be spotted. Across the street from a two-story restaurant, they noticed a huge yacht that looked to be loading up supplies.

"I bet that's the one they are heading out on." Luke said excitedly.

"Let's get tables up at the restaurant across the way where we can get a good vantage point and discuss our plan of action, "Bobby said. "Doesn't look they will be heading out anytime soon."

They parked the car and quickly and quietly headed up to the restaurant. They specifically asked for seating in the upstairs dining room. It was a warm night and the large plastic vinyl walls were still rolled up for the season.

The group put two tables together and felt very confident they were out of view of the men on the boat. They ordered their meals and discussed their next moves.

The men once again brought up the case from the beginning. Bobby and Luke wanted to know who was the one that called them that first night.

"That was me, I confess." Avery said with a sheepish grin. "I had finally found out who had my safe. Big Al's men had stolen it from the house that Jack was operating it out of. He was furious when he found out. I knew I had to get you two up there quickly because no one would have suspected two innocent kids coming across it." Avery replied.

"Dad, was that cruise really a vacation or a surveillance?" Luke asked.

"Both actually, "he smiled. "But I wanted your mother to think it was something we set up to relax. She will understand once this is all wrapped up."

Mr. Robinson's cellphone rang, and he answered it. "Great Frank. We are sitting across the marina in a restaurant upstairs. We have a full vantage point of the yacht we are certain Jack is on board." he said.

After discussing their plan of attack, he hung and let the group know their next steps.

"The FBI will be here shortly. We need to have a positive idea about Jack and that is indeed the yacht he is on. "he added.

"I'll go." Bobby spoke up.

"Me too." Luke chimed in.

"I agree with the boys. It's now or never, otherwise Jack will get away." Doug added.

Mr. Robinson thought for a moment of the right plan of action. He didn't want his sons to walk into a trap. He knew how dangerous Jack was and didn't want them hurt. They ate their meals all the while keeping an eye on the yacht. For almost an hour there was no sighting of Jack, or his henchman and they could barely make out any lights on the yacht. Mr.

Robinson had informed the restaurant manager what they were doing, and he readily agreed to let them stay at their table.

After the group finished the meal, they continued to discuss their plan.

"They must be waiting for complete darkness to move on out. "Lee spoke up.

"Time to move out. "Bobby said.

"Okay, but you boys must be careful. We will need some sort of sign that you got onto the boat safely without being spotted. "he said.

"We will turn on a cellphone flashlight briefly to let you know we got there. Let's go Luke and make our way to the water. "Bobby said.

"I'm coming with you. I know Jack's whole plan and you will need me for backup." Doug said.

The three of them made their way out the back door of the restaurant and down to the waterfront area. They used their cellphone cameras as binoculars and peered across the way.

"How do we get over there without being seen?" Luke asked his brother.

Bobby looked all around for some type of small boat they could steal and quietly row their way across the water. It was getting darker, and the lights of the marina were in the distance.

They were protected by the darkness of the shoreline. Bobby looked to his right and saw a twenty-foot boat approaching the marina. It slowly made its way to the yacht and two men unloaded three wooden crates.

Soon after, the boat skimmed the waters and headed to the shoreline not far from where the boys crouched down low in the tall high grass.

"How are we going to get to the yacht?" Luke nervously asked his brother.

Bobby thought for a moment. He noticed at the back of the small boat a huge tarp that was covering something up at the back.

"If we can get down there, we can hide under that tarp. The driver must be picking up some supplies for the yacht." Bobby responded.

They noticed no one else in the boat and all three decided it was now or never to get onto the boat. They crouched down low and worked their way through the tall high grass using it as a shield. The narrow path led down to the back of the boat. Bobby entered the water quietly and got to the back side and slithered up the small ladder. He peered over the edge and didn't see anyone onboard standing there. He quietly worked his way under the tarp. Luke and Doug soon followed and all three were soon safely hidden from sight.

"Make sure your phones are silenced, "Bobby warned them. "I'm going to text Dad to let him know we are hidden under the tarp." He texted his father and got a thumbs up emoji as a reply.

"The FBI better hurry or they are out of here tonight." Doug whispered.

After about fifteen minutes of agonizing silence, the boys heard heavy footsteps along the wooden planks of the dock walkway. The men entered the boat, and a huge thud was heard.

"Careful with those boxes Marty. "a husky voice shouted out.

"Think we have enough food to get us there?" came another voice.

"Jack said the restaurant manager hooked us up really good." The man replied.

"Let's get out of here before someone spots us." said Marty.

The boat engines came to life and made their way quietly

back across the water as light rain began to fall. Lightning strikes appeared on the horizon and a storm was brewing.

The boat again docked at the yacht and both men helped to get the boxes up on board.

When the coast was clear, Bobby peaked out from under the tarp. He saw no one on the boat and only saw a few lights visible on the yacht.

"Let's move out quietly, "He whispered to the others. He texted his father to say they had made it.

Again, came the thumbs up emoji reply.

Bobby led the way and the three of them crawled along the bottom of the boat to keep from being detected. They sat with their backs to the boat and listened for any sounds from above. Bobby turned around and slowly raised his head to look up at the yacht. He noticed one man was signaling a light across the water towards the restaurant. The light was morse code as it flickered off and on.

"Someone's signaling to shore." He whispered, lowering his body.

"He must be signaling for confirmation." Luke whispered back.

From on shore a light flashed once, then twice, then completely went dark.

Bobby slowly raised his head again and noticed the coast was clear.

"Come on." Bobby said.

The three of them made their way to the front of the boat and used the ladder to slowly climb onboard the yacht. They noticed the boat deck was clear and they quickly hoisted themselves overboard. They made their way back and peered around the corner. Bobby slowly edged his way to the glass door leading to the interior of the boat. Two men were inside and conversing amongst themselves. Bobby held up his right hand in a peace sign to indicate there were two men inside. Doug kept an eye out behind him to make sure they weren't being followed.

"Where is Jack?" Luke whispered.

"He must be below deck with his gang making last minute preparations." Bobby said.

The weather started to worsen quickly as the rain began to get heavier and the thunder and lightning became more frequent and louder.

The boys heard splashing sounds coming from behind the boat. A rowboat approached the back of the yacht.

"More of his men?" Doug asked.

"It's possible." Bobby said.

"We got to get out here and hide." Luke said panicking.

They found a quick hiding spot behind a collapsible boat. From there they had a clear vantage point to hear all that was taking place. Bobby decided to take photos and he whispered to Luke to record the conversation. Luke got out his phone and started to take video of what was taking place.

The rowboat docked and two more men came on board in a panic.

"What's the rush?" One of the men said.

"Feds on their way, we gotta scram!" The man shouted.

"What are you talking about Freddy?" The other man said.

"We've been watched from across the water this whole time from a restaurant."

He pointed across the water.

All four men made their way to the starboard side of ship.

"There, see that restaurant?" He pointed. "We've been getting tips from the manager about a suspicious group that has been sitting at window side table this whole time." he said.

"So? They could just be enjoying a dinner, stop getting jacked up." The man responded angrily.

"I'm telling you, something's fishy."

Bobby glanced down at his phone and noticed a red siren emoji. That meant everything was about to get crazy. He showed it to Luke and Doug.

The weather was suddenly turning violent. Lightning strikes were turning bright, and the thunder was deafening.

Suddenly, Jack appeared at the door and demanded to know what was going on.

"Boss, we got trouble." Freddy said nervously.

"Shut up." He replied angrily. "We are heading out now, man your posts."

"But boss, the weather is….." He couldn't finish his thoughts as Jack sent a crushing right hook to his jaw. The man collapsed onto the floor of the yacht. "Get rid of him, "Jack ordered. The man was lifted up and carried to the back of the boat and sent overboard. The boys didn't move, and the look of horror was shown on their faces.

"Boss, look!" He shouted.

Coming up the waterway from opposite directions were two patrol boats.

"Everybody scram!" Jack shouted. "Lance, come with me." The two men ran to the end of the boat and descended the ladder into the small rowboat.

"Boss, you can't leave us here." Freddy screamed.

"Sucks to be you," came a creepy laugh.

The patrol boats suddenly lit up the night sky with blue flashing lights.

"We can't risk him disappearing into the night." Bobby said to Luke.

The rowboat carrying Jack and Lance slowly rowed away

under the cover of darkness. As it made it's way along the shore it used the broken branches as cover.

The patrol boats reached the yacht and agents poured over the side in two-by-two cover formation.

"Get your hands up now!" ordered one of the agents.

From the interior of the yacht shots were fired shattering the double glass sliding doors.

Agents took cover and returned the fire. Bobby, Luke and Doug remained hidden by the collapsible boat.

The men gave up and raised their hands. "We surrender."

The agents slowly approached the doorway as more men came outside. The gang was handcuffed and ordered to sit Indian style along the edge of the boat.

More agents came from the front of the boat and made their way quickly into the interior of the boat. Four more men were led out in handcuffs. Mr. Robinson appeared at the back of the boat with Tony and Lee.

"Dad, Jack got away. He's in a rowboat just offshore." Bobby yelled.

"Agent Thomas, get two men back to the patrol boat and scour the area." He barked.

"Yes sir, right away." Came the reply.

"We'll join them." Luke joined in.

The patrol boat moved slowly through the water with their high-powered searchlight scanning the shore. The blue patrol lights were bouncing off the trees. They noticed a small rowboat hidden in the brush.

Put your hands up!" the agent ordered. "And don't make a move!"

As the patrol boat closed in on Jack's boat, Lance jumped overboard and quickly scampered onto the shore. He had trouble getting his footing on the muddy shore.

Bobby jumped in the water to try and catch him. Lance

regained his footing and made it up the hill. He ran at a fast sprint along the grassy field. Bobby was right behind him in hot pursuit.

Lance suddenly stopped, turned and caught Bobby with a right hook to jaw. He stumbled to the ground and Lance began to race across the field.

Bobby caught up to Lance with a flying linebacker style tackle and pinned him to the ground.

The two got up and Lance attempted a second punch to Bobby's face. But this time he ducked and sent a full crushing punch to Lance's gut. He doubled over in pain and fell to the ground.

The agents handcuffed Lance and brought him aboard the patrol boat.

Meanwhile, Luke had chased Jack up the same hill. Jack was much faster than Luke and had gained a considerable distance between them. Jack stumbled after getting his foot caught in a hole in the ground and winced in pain. Luke caught up to him in a hurry and tackled Jack to the ground. Both wrestled around in the grass trading blows to the face.

Luke was knocked down. He regained his footing, shaking off the cobwebs and forcefully pinned Jack down and handcuffed him.

Agents soon followed and Jack and Lance were taken into custody. The FBI had rounded up all the gang and everyone was seated on the boat.

Avery finally came on board the ship and walked up to Jack and just stared at him.

"Jack, why did you do it.?"

"I got nothing to say to you. I'm going to plead innocent, and my lawyer is going to have a field day with you." He replied angrily.

"Lance, you want to tell me everything?" Mr. Robinson said as he approached him.

Lance looked in Jack's direction but said nothing.

"We can make it easier on you Lance if you cooperate." He added.

"You aren't getting anything out of us." Jack shouted.

"That's not exactly a smart thing to do, "Agent Thomas interjected. "One of these guys is going to cooperate with us sooner or later."

Bobby and Luke got up and approached Jack.

"It's okay Jack, we got everything we need." Bobby said holding up their cellphones.

"Video and photo proof that put's you behind bars for a long time."

Jack shot them a nasty look but said nothing.

"Take them away fellows." Mr. Robinson ordered.

The men were taken away and the boys all hugged each other and their father. They were saddened to know the case had come to an end. They wouldn't have to wait long when *The Case of the Hidden Gems* would come along soon.

Printed in the United States
by Baker & Taylor Publisher Services